MW01035915

CARMELLA'S FATE

by

Paul Blades

Previously published:

Vol. I	Maddy becomes a Ponygirl
Vol. II	The Training of a Ponygirl
Vol. III	Ponygirl Champion
Vol. IV	Ponygirl Summer
Vol. V	Ponygirl Love
Vol. VI	Ponygirl Season
Vol. VII	Ponygirl Gambit
Vol. VIII	Ponygirl Pleasures

Watch for publication of the other books in the Maddy Saga:

| Vol. IX | Ponygirl Peril |
| Vol. X | Ponygirl's Choice |

Other books by Paul Blades:

Klitzman's Isle
Klitzman's Empire
Klitzman's Paradise
Klitzman's Pawn Part One
Klitzman's Pawn Part Two
Slaver's Dozen- A Tale of Klitzman's Isle
The Taking of Cheryl Part One
The Taking of Cheryl Part Two: Slaver's Bait
Comfort Girl No. 4
Sacrifice to the Emerald God
The Blue Cantina: Anna's Surrender
The Warlord's Concubine, Books 1, 2, 3 and 4
Dreams and Desires, Books 1 and 2

CHAPTER ONE

The bright Mediterranean sun sparkled on the waters as far as the eye could see. Jeb sat under a bright, yellow canopy on the foredeck of the yacht. It was 10:30, but the Prince had not yet appeared. Jeb had breakfasted on fruit and a kind of honey cake and was now sipping his second cup of coffee. Unsure as to his current status, he was nervous about this first meeting with the Prince. He was worried most of all that somehow the Prince had found out who he really was, that he was searching for Carmella. Jeb was a gambler by nature and he was gambling all on his ability to deceive the powers that be in Calipha, and on somehow figuring a way to save her.

Finally the Prince appeared, dressed casually, in tan pants and a bright yellow short sleeved sport shirt. Jeb had been unsure whether the Prince would be bedecked in full Arab regalia, the flowing robes, the rope encircled headdress, a chained slave in tow. But here he was in the guise of a Harvard sportsman.

"Mr. Turner, I am sorry to keep you waiting. It is good to meet you at last."

Jeb stood. "It's my honor, your Highness."

"Please sit. Would you like more coffee?" the Prince asked.

"No, thank you," Jeb replied, I'm already on my second cup."

"Did you enjoy your night's rest?"

Now that was a loaded question. Jeb hesitated briefly before answering. How did one say that he had enjoyed practically the best sex of his life with two nubile, young slave girls? Surely the Prince knew that he had been granted the full hospitality of the house, so to speak. But Jeb could not quite get around the thought of casually discussing the reality of human slavery with one of the world's most prolific practitioners.

"It was highly unusual," Jeb finally managed to blurt out. "I mean…"

"Oh yes, your first encounter with one of the principal products of my country. Do not be embarrassed, Mr. Turner. In our culture, women exist to be enjoyed by men."

"Yes, quite, your Highness, but, I mean that…" Jeb stammered.

"Paul, may I call you Paul?" the Prince asked.

"Certainly, you Highness," Jeb responded.

"Paul, I must know that you will be comfortable working closely with me. Female slavery is as natural to me as owning a horse or a dog or any other animal that can bring me pleasure." The Prince paused to pour himself a glass of orange juice.

He continued. "You were not consulted in advance as to the details of your accommodations because I wanted to immerse you in the sea in which you will swim if you become my financial confidant. I must know whether you will blanch at my lifestyle or not. Can we do business together or should we put you ashore at the next opportunity?"

Jeb thought his answer over carefully. There was really only one answer he could give. Only one answer if he was to realize his goal: entry into Calipha. But, he knew that any Westerner would have discomfort at the thought of slavery, not to mention a personal involvement in it. So he could not play this hand too strong or too weak.

"Let me say this, your Highness," Jeb said slowly, measuring each word. "I have been brought up to think that slavery is evil, wrong. Frankly, right now I really don't give a damn, if you will excuse the vulgarity."

The Prince laughed, "Vulgarity excused!" he exclaimed.

Jeb continued. "I don't give a damn because I see this job as the opportunity of a lifetime. I know I can make you a lot of money, your Highness, and I also know that if I do, I will be very well rewarded. This is my shot at the good life, and any qualms I might have about the fate of women who I don't know and who I could care less about is definitely outweighed by that goal."

The Prince looked at Jeb thoughtfully. Jeb waited while his words were being measured. Did he pass or fail?

"Paul, I believe you," the Prince finally said. "And let me say that I will be happy working with you."

Jeb felt exuberant. He had passed.

"Look at it this way, if it makes any difference to you," the Prince continued. "Your country is the richest in the world, the richest in history. And what is that wealth dependant on? It depends on the exploitation of human labor. It depends on the existence of men and women all over the world who will work for pittances merely to keep their body and souls together. Are they not slaves? Do they have any real choice in how their lives are led? And when their rulers imprison them, shoot them, or worse, when they rebel, are they not being treated as slaves would? My country exploits the women of other lands. And I'm sure you are aware, because you've done your homework, none of them volunteer to become slaves. But did the peons of South America or the native mineworkers in South Africa volunteer to be poor and exploited? No. Of course not."

Jeb could see that this line of self justification of the Prince was well rehearsed. He probably believed it.

The Prince continued, "My country exploits a relatively miniscule number of women, a tiny fraction of the world's population. Your country and the other countries of the West exploit hundreds of millions. Your system cannot exist without it."

The Prince paused and caught himself. "But we are not here on this beautiful Mediterranean morning to discuss politics. We are here to enjoy ourselves and to get to know one another, eh?"

"Of course, your Highness," Jeb agreed, happy to leave the minefield of political science.

"So it's settled. You will work for me. My man, Rashid, will brief you on my major holdings and the sources of my cash flow. You will advise me on an investment strategy. I have set aside an office and a computer for you, with Internet, of course. We have subscribed to all of the principal on-line sources of financial information and news. You will have plenty of time to prepare your brief to me. Let's say, a preliminary summary and assessment in one week, okay?"

Jeb was stunned. A week! He did not have time to protest as Rashid appeared, magically, at the mention of his name.

"Mr. Turner, if you please, I will show you to your working quarters," the trim and polite major domo interjected.

"Sure, show me the way," Jeb replied. He followed Rashid below decks.

The Prince watched Jeb leave and then rose from his chair and strolled leisurely along the deck. He recalled wistfully the pleasurable service he had received last night from two delightful, well trained slaves. He had an hour to kill before he had to make his telephone calls. He had many threads to keep track of as the head of a small empire. Deals had to be made, subordinates required instruction. He looked forward to a little recreation before doing his business for the day.

Entering the reception room, where he had delighted in the enslavement of the two young women the night before, he saw that, as usual, his instructions had been carried out to the letter. Both of the young women were there. They were standing, and each had her hands fastened behind her back, her wrists, in turn, affixed to a chain that descended from the ceiling. Their arms were pulled up tight causing them to lean forward. Their breasts dangled free, swaying gently as they recorded the subtle movements of the ship over the sea. Their legs were spread by bars affixed to their ankles and large weights hung from their nipples, fastened by alligator clips. Both girls wore leather hoods designed to block out all light and sound. Their mouths were covered.

He silently approached the two trussed up women. Standing behind them, he reached between their legs and addressed the gash that lay between. Both women jumped with surprise. The blonde gave a little squeal, almost imperceptible due to the efficiency of the hard rubber cock in her mouth and the leather base that sealed her lips. The Prince stroked the slits gently, his finger lightly teasing the buds at the apex. He waited until they were both fully lubricated before stepping away and moving to a spot in front of them. The Prince clapped his hands and a white-coated attendant appeared. Short, diminutive in build, dark of skin and hair, he bowed deferentially to the Prince as he awaited his instructions.

"Remove the masks," the Prince told him. He attendant quickly and efficiently removed the hood from the dark Jamaican and then the thin Englishwoman. The women remained gagged, but their vision was restored and they both looked up with trepidation at this monster who had treated them so cruelly the night before. They had spent the night caged below decks. While there, they had been fitted with thick leather collars and leather bands around their ankles and wrists. They had not been fed, although they had been allowed water. The hoods had been on all night.

"Well, ladies, I hope you enjoyed your accommodations. I don't want it ever said that I failed to be hospitable to my guests." The Prince's voice was teasing and light, almost farcical. But the two abject women were in no mood to be entertained. They both recalled the Prince's promise of punishments from the night before.

"Now I have some activities planned for you that will, I think, enliven your morning. I haven't forgotten your misbehavior and I do intend to give you lessons in obedience."

He lifted the head of the blonde. "For you I think twenty-five lashes across the breasts with the cane.'

The girl, Vicki, trembled at the Prince's touch. The raising of her head caused her arms to be pulled downwards, increasing the strain on her shoulders from her already painful posture. Her eyes telegraphed what she would have said if she were able to speak, pleading for mercy.

"But before we administer what you deserve," the Prince continued, "I think a little preparation is called for." He turned to the attendant. "Take this whore and lash her to the deck. Make sure she is in a position to enjoy the beautiful rays of the sun, but just across the breasts. Cover the rest of her." He turned towards the blond woman. "When your breasts have burned a bright pink, then we'll have our little soiree."

The attendant released Vicki's arms from the chain behind her and freed her ankles from the bar that had separated them. After removing the nipple clamps, he began to lead her from the room. Vicki pulled back, resisting, wailing and pleading from behind her gag.

The Prince reached over and grabbed her by the hair, twisting her head sideways and then up so that she could look into his eyes. His eyes were afire, his face red. "Do you not understand what you are?" he bellowed. "You are my property, a walking three holed beast! You will endure what suffering I choose to mete out to you, you will serve me as it pleases me!"

The girl's eyes were wide with fear. Nothing in her life had prepared her for this. She was too frightened even to cry.

"You have earned yourself twenty-five more lashes," the Prince told her, his voice lowered now, but filled with steel edged firmness. To the attendant he spoke, "When her tits are nice and red, turn her over and let her white ass feel the heat of the sun. Oil her up well so that her skin will burn quickly."

The attendant, having regained Vicki's arm, pulled at her to escort her from the room. She followed his lead meekly now, abject in her despair.

The Prince turned to the tawny skinned Jamaican, still bent over, her breasts swaying as her chest heaved in fear and anticipation. He circled her, taking in her gracious curves, the taut muscles of her thighs, the roundness and fullness of her buttocks. "Oh, I have something special planned for you," the Prince taunted the frightened woman. He ran his hands along the cheeks of her ass, along her sides and then, as he stood behind her, grabbed her breasts and pulled her body into his.

"What wonderful mounds you have," he said as he removed the saw-toothed clips from her nipples and then took the soft and ample orbs into his large, soft hands. He rubbed them, pushing them up into the helpless woman's chest. He pushed them together, squeezing them tight, causing a slight moan of protest to rise from the woman's gagged mouth. The moan grew louder, yet still was feint, as he pinched the nipples where the alligator clips had made her flesh raw. His cock was engorged and hard. He rubbed it against the woman's ass, between the crack that divided it.

"Do you feel that, whore?" he said, referring to his prick. "You have made me quite hot. I think that I will take a little diversion before we get to the main event."

The Prince motioned to the attendant and issued a curt order in Arabic. While the attendant ran to the cabinet in the wall to retrieve something, the Prince freed his hefty, rock hard cock from his pants. He spoke to the woman brazenly displayed before him.

"What was your name again?" he asked playfully. "Oh, yes, it was Yolanda, wasn't it?" He paused as if expecting an answer. "Well, Yolanda, since this brazen display of your flesh has excited me, it's only fair, isn't it, that you assist me in obtaining some relief?" He reached and pulled her head back by her hair, short, curly black hair, just long enough to permit a handful to be grasped.

"I said, 'Isn't it?'" The Prince's voice was now louder, transmitting more than a hint of cruelty. The girl's eyes darted back and forth as she sought some way to assuage the Prince's rising anger. She mewed at her gag, hoping that if her attempt at affirmance of the Prince's suggestion was understood, that somehow his drift towards an irrational cruelty could be abated.

"Have you ever been fucked in the ass, Yolanda?" the Prince asked, his voice modulated a tone lower, apparently satisfied by Yolanda's attempt to respond. "I know that you prefer a woman's touch," continued the Prince, "but alas, it is no longer you who will decide who will enjoy your body."

As the Prince was speaking to Yolanda, the attendant had produced a small tube of gel. The Prince nodded to him, stroking his manhood in anticipation. The attendant took a small squeeze of lubricant onto his hand and applied it to the star that sat at the center of Yolanda's ass. Yolanda squirmed at his touch ineffectually.

"You see Yolanda, since you have abjured the proper use of your cunt, I feel it is only proper that you make available the other avenues of pleasure open to a man. In fact, I'm contemplating having your fuck hole sewn up so that no one will be tempted to enter that despoiled organ."

Yolanda had no doubt that if that was what the Prince wanted, it would be done. As the Prince's hands found their way once more to her buttocks, she steeled herself for the assault that would soon follow. She determined that she would not resist the inevitable, that she would attempt to relax her sphincter muscles, permitting a softer entry. What she did not calculate was the effect of a thick cock like the Prince's on her small, puckered anus, the tearing of her skin as the point of entry was forced wide, the burning that would result from the movement of the hard sword of flesh as it was dragged across the torn tissue.

"Now, my dear," the Prince said to Yolanda as he pushed the tip of his cock around the entranceway to her bowels, "you have been lubricated, so this might not hurt as much as it would otherwise, but do not think that it is for your benefit. I just don't want my cock abraded by the dry lips of your shithole. You and I have a lot of work to do with this tool of mine and we want to keep it fresh and ready for action, don't we?" The Prince laughed at his jibe at Yolanda's expense. His laugh turned into a grin as he pushed the head of his cock past the soft lips of Yolanda's rear entrance.

Even lubricated, the going was difficult. Yolanda moaned and whined behind her gag as the pain of the forced entry of her ass shot through her. But the Prince was in ecstasy. The tight outer rim of Yolanda's anus pressed hard on his dick, her bowels were hot and soft. Slowly, but surely, the Prince sank his cock into Yolanda up to the hilt. He withdrew it slowly, enjoying the drag of the still tight muscles of her hole around the shaft of his cock. He repeated the exercise, his cock absorbing the heat of Yolanda's steaming bowels.

As the Prince pumped his manhood into her rear passage, Yolanda began to feel a strange tingling in her lower belly. The sensation of the rigid member in her ass, rubbing across her fractured tissue, delivered an echo in her pussy. She did not want it, but she could not hold back the incipient passion that was aroused by the Prince's long, slow strokes. Involuntarily, she squeezed her anus muscles tight, seeking a firmer purchase on the bar of iron that pierced her.

When the Prince finally allowed the heat of his loins to overcome his almost detached enjoyment of Yolanda's ass, his strokes became harder, more determined. Yolanda's passion grew as she tried to push her ass backwards in unison with the movement of the Prince's cock. Against her will, she was being fucked in her ass, a thing she had never contemplated as likely to happen to her, one who had disdained men. But now, her blood was on the boil as the outrageous act that was being perpetrated on her drove her towards an unwanted, but mighty climax. As she felt the Prince's seed spilled into her guts, she exploded, grunting and shuddering, oblivious to her surroundings, her personal predicament.

His passion abated, the Prince pulled his cock from Yolanda's ass and stood back. Her sexual gratification did not go unnoticed. "This slut will wear her slavery well," the Prince thought.

The attendant brought the Prince a small wet towel to clean off his manhood. When he was done, he replaced his now soft tool into his pants. He signaled for refreshment and an attendant, apparently waiting in the wings, rushed in with a tray on which sat a pitcher of deep orange mango juice and a glass. The attendant poured the juice into the glass and handed it to the Prince. He drank from the glass eagerly.

He turned to the bound and panting Jamaican and spoke, "You are a good ass fuck my dear. You may expect to be well used there."

Yolanda was overwhelmed by shame. She had let a man drive her to orgasm through the rape of her most private place. She was experiencing sensations so strange to her that she thought that she might possibly be going mad.

After savoring his drink, the Prince signaled to the attendant to prepare Yolanda for her beating. The man released Yolanda's hands from her back and fastened them in front, still attached to the chain that ran from the ceiling. He then detached the bar from her ankles and, after drawing another chain down from the ceiling, affixed it to her right ankle. He went to the wall and pushed a button, causing the chain around Yolanda's ankle to rise.

Yolanda had docilely let the attendant manipulate her. She was overcome with the fact that she had allowed this mongrel of a man drive her to pleasure. She had never received pleasure from a cock before and never wanted to. What was happening to her?

The tension on her right ankle surprised the contemplative girl. As her right leg began to rise she was forced to try and maintain her balance with her left. She fell backwards, saved from hitting the floor by the chain that held her wrists. Slowly her ankle rose until her leg was virtually perpendicular to the floor. The Prince admired her well-toned legs stretched out to their extreme. He stepped near Yolanda and ran his hand down the length of her upright leg, starting at her ankle and down to the center point. The attendant affixed Yolanda's other ankle to a hook embedded in the floor.

Yolanda's pussy was wide open and fully exposed. The Prince ran his hand over the juicy, soft lips. It was still moist and soft from Yolanda's climax, her feminine odors delighting the Prince's olfactory senses.

"Now we can get down to business, young lady," he said. "You were quite an inconvenience last night and I'm afraid you earned yourself a good thrashing. I'm going to remove your gag now because I want to hear your screams of pain. I'm afraid that the earnest wailing of a tortured female is an immensely pleasurable experience for me. So your whipping will serve a dual purpose: instructing you as to the consequences of bad behavior and allowing me sensual delight."

Signaling the attendant to remove Yolanda's gag, the Prince took himself to his throne-like chair. He signaled again and his bodyguard, whose ubiquitous presence was concealed by his ability to blend in with the background, stepped forward. The man was a wall of solid muscle, yet he was limber and quick. His movements were deliberate, calculating, but accomplished, with the grace of a tiger. Strength and determination oozed from the hulking man. And he, too, enjoyed the screams that were produced by the assiduous application of pain to female flesh.

Yolanda, knowing what was coming, tried to hold back her sobs as she saw the guard remove from the wall cabinet the whip that had been used on Vicki the night before. The man cracked it in the air, causing a loud "snap". Yolanda jumped at the sound, anticipating the kiss of the leather strap on her inner thighs. She was determined not to cry out, not to beg for mercy. She was strong; she would outlast them.

The first blow struck across her right thigh, midway between her hip and her knee. The pain was searing, unlike anything she had ever known. She bit her lip, expecting another blow to follow. But the guard was practiced at his art. He knew that half of the experience of being whipped was the anticipation of the pain. Terror increased incrementally as the punishment was extended.

After about twenty seconds another lashing blow was delivered, this time mid-thigh on the left leg. Yolanda stiffened in pain, her resolve not to beg and plead for deliverance from this experience weakening. The guard knew what he was about and the next blow was a snap of the end of the whip, cracking like the snapping of a piece of wood. The blow landed at the center of Yolanda's sex. The shock of the blow sent a wave of pain through Yolanda's body. Her pussy stung with the effects of the snapping of the end of the lash. As she realized that her most tender place was not to be spared, her resolve not to cry out, not to plead for an end to her torture, all but disappeared.

"Ahhhhhhh!" she cried, her voice shattering the silence of the room. It was the first time a sound had emanated from her lips since she had been brought aboard. "Oh, god, oh, god, please don't do this to me! I'll be good, I'll be your slave, I'll do anything, but please, please, don't whip me!" Her voice was high toned and plaintive, panic seeping in to her expressions.

A smile crossed the Prince's face. "She didn't last long, now, did she?" he thought to himself. He was enjoying the spectacle before him. He was assessing the full worth of the dark skinned beauty who screamed and writhed helplessly, her legs spread as wide as her body would permit, and then some. "There is nothing like a good lashing to bring out a woman's true character," he mused.

Four quick blows in succession drove Yolanda over the brink. She cried and moaned as loud as she could make her voice heard. She protested her innocence, promised a plethora of sexual acts, asked fate or God or whoever she was hoping would hear her, what had she done to merit such cruelty?

Twenty five times the whip was applied forcefully to her outstretched thighs and to her sex. Her voice was just a steady wail by the time that the torture ended, lowering slowly in volume as she prayed that her torment was at an end. The Prince was well satisfied. It was an immensely rewarding experience. His cock was hard again and, he thought to himself, warranted further attention from this sweating, moaning bitch.

CHAPTER TWO

Jeb had been conscientiously attending to the Prince's financial records when he heard a faint wail coming from above decks. At first he thought he was hearing things, maybe the whine of a winch, or the calling of some exotic bird. But as the wail persisted, its pitch rising steadily, he knew that it could be only one thing. Some female was being tortured.

All at once his perspective on the obsequious come-liness of the two women who had so eagerly serviced him last night and this morning was altered dramatically. He realized for the first time the role that fear and terror had played in molding those young women into virtual automatons of pleasure. His throat constricted as he pictured Carmella suffering as the unknown woman whose tortured voice he could hear was undoubtedly suffering. He steeled himself in his resolve to save her. Nothing meant more than that. He could not help the woman whose voice he heard, who was suffering some extreme of abuse that he could not imagine. He could not help any of them, not the girl whose suffering he could hear, or the suffering of the servile women who had already crossed his path. But he was determined that he could, and would, help Carmella, no matter what he had to do.

At about one o'clock, Rashid came to call him for lunch. He rose from his studies and followed Rashid above decks. As he walked down the starboard side, he spied a small bundle, wrapped and tied to the deck. As he got closer, he realized that it was a woman and that she was covered with some type of tarp, all but her ass, that is. As he passed the woman, he could see the glistening of oil on her backside. The skin was turning pink. He could hear soft moans from beneath the tarp.

Rashid pulled him along towards amidships where the dining room of the yacht was situated. He sat down to a plate of fresh, tender tilapia, covered with a nut and honey sauce. Rashid produced a bottle of dry, chilled, white wine and poured Jeb a glass. Jeb could not help contrast the sumptuousness of the meal he was about to ingest with the terrible treatment of the woman who had been screaming and the odd punishment that had apparently been allocated to the woman under the tarp. Although he had been almost put off of his feed by this absurd inequity of experiences, he knew that he had to demonstrate his ability to inure himself to the sufferings around him if he was ever to gain the Prince's trust and confidence.

But for the presence of Rashid, who sat opposite him, Jeb ate alone at the huge, dark, mahogany table. It was inlaid with decorative tiles, each containing a primitive drawing of sexual congress, or a lascivious display of a cartoon-like lady's charms. Only a cartoon woman could accomplish the positions achieved by these illustrated females. Only the most cartoonish of women would have breasts and thighs the size of the women in the drawings and only the most fortunate of men the girth and length of the sexual organs displayed. Nonetheless, the presence of the tiles was erotic and gave Jeb some discomfort as he sat silently eating his midday repast.

With real and apparent eagerness, Jeb savored the fine tastes of the wine and the fish. He paused only to observe a young blond girl, apparently in tears, being led past the portholes of the dining room and towards the bow. She was led by one of the many small, slightly built attendants he had seen, the one who had served his breakfast, the one that served him now. Slaves were apparently for fucking and torture, not to be used as servants in any other respects.

He knew better than to interrogate Rashid about the fate of the woman or why she had been so harshly punished. But he needed to talk about something. "Where's the Prince?" he asked Rashid.

Rashid looked over at Jeb stonily. "The Prince is engaged," he answered coldly. "What he does is no concern of ours."

"Oh, of course, I didn't mean to..." Jeb stammered.

Rashid smiled. "You have much to learn Mr. Turner. It will come with time. In any case, after lunch the Prince would like you to come to the reception room. He wishes to learn what you have concluded so far from your examination."

"But I've only just started to...." Jeb attempted to protest.

"Nonsense, Mr. Turner," Rashid went on, waiving his hand. "You have an expert's eye. I am sure that the Prince does not expect a full statement of findings, but he wants to see what your impressions are, to measure your acuity."

"Well I can give him some generalized suggestions," Jeb replied. "But more than that...."

"Excellent, Mr. Turner, excellent. That is what the Price desires, just some generalities. After all, we did not meet you until yesterday and for all we know your professed expertise in financial matters could be puffery, a ruse."

Jeb felt his throat dry up. The fish he was chewing turned to chalk in his mouth, his stomach turned. "A, a, ruse?" he managed to drawl out.

"Oh, I don't mean anything particular by it, but you have to realize how careful the Prince has to be. Many

Western governments, although they tolerate my country's peculiar institutions, would like to infiltrate our country, gain knowledge about our fiscal procedures. Knowledge is power, Mr. Turner, as I am sure you are aware."

"Yes, of course," Jeb replied anxious to regain his equilibrium. "Well I've eaten about enough, maybe we should get going?" he suggested to Rashid.

"Oh, no, Mr. Turner, it is not yet time. Have some coffee, a sweet roll perhaps?"

Jeb declined the dessert but accepted the coffee. Like everything else he had consumed since coming aboard the Prince's incomparably luxurious yacht, it was delectable.

After finishing the coffee and some more small talk with Rashid, Jeb observed an attendant appear and whisper to Rashid. "Ah," Rashid exclaimed, "the Prince awaits you in the reception room. The servant will show you the way."

Jeb rose and followed the small, white-coated man forward. As he entered the reception room, he took in its splendid furnishings. He saw the Prince sitting at a small table towards the forward end of the room. He stood to greet Jeb.

"Good of you to come, Paul. I just want to see if you have any thoughts after reviewing my portfolio this morning," he said.

"As a matter of fact I do have some thoughts, you highness, I..." Jeb halted. In the middle of the room he took in the form of the blond girl he had seen earlier. She was standing on her tiptoes, her arms affixed to a chain that came down from the ceiling. She wore a gag in her mouth. She was apparently struggling to keep her weight off of her toes as her hands were pulling on the chain to lighten the impact of her weight. She had a band of red colored skin across her breasts. The rest of her was marble white.

As Jeb's eyes adjusted to the relative darkness of the room, he then noticed a shapely dark skinned woman kneeling on the floor behind the blonde one. She was also gagged. Both women wore a collar and leather bracelets around their wrists and ankles. The dark woman had her knees spread open and her hands behind her head, elbows out. He could clearly see the apex of her thighs, her black thatch divided by prominent pink lips. Her breasts jutted proudly and the distended nipples were surrounded by large, dark, almost black aureoles.

"Oh, you have noticed my latest acquisitions," the Prince commented. "This one is Vicki." He pointed to the blonde. "And the comely wench kneeling so submissively is Yolanda." The Prince stood and walked over to the cruelly strung up pale, blonde woman.

"This one is awaiting punishment," he said as he rubbed his hands across her breasts. Jeb could see the woman stiffen as the Prince abraded her obviously tender skin.

"Punishment?" Jeb queried. "For what?"

"Last night she was so frightened at the prospect of a whipping that she pissed herself, right here on my rug! Now we can't have that, can we?" The Prince emphasized his point by squeezing Vicki's cheeks and shaking her head. Vicki's eyes were wide with fear and anticipation of the pain she knew was yet to come. She tried to gurgle an answer through her gag.

"Surely, you met them coming in on the launch," the Prince said.

"On the launch?" Jeb thought. There was no one on the launch but him, the bodyguards and the two burkha-covered ladies. But then the horror of it all came to him. He had been witness to the kidnapping of these two now helpless women. One of them had tried to speak to him.

What was she trying to say? Was it a desperate call for help? The man had silenced her.

Jeb tried to regain his composure. "Oh, yeah, I remember them. But I thought that they were members of your family, they were all dressed up as…"

"Yes, all dressed up as Arab women. I know. What better way to smuggle a helpless captive aboard. Anyone who had seen them would have thought the same as you. But let's discuss our business first and then I shall administer a beating to the blonde one for our pleasure."

Jeb had a hard time, at first, concentrating his mind on business. But after a few minutes, he was in the swing of things, his mind off of the two naked women behind his back. He pointed out to the Prince how he was losing interest on some of his cash by its delayed transfer. The banks were earning a "vig" on the money as it lay dormant, waiting the 'clearance' of a wire transfer. On an average balance of accounts of several million dollars, and transfers of hundreds of thousands of dollars at a time, this amounted to a good piece of change. "And the banks are really screwing you on the interest rates," he told the Prince. He explained how he could pressure the banks to give him a better deal on interest. "An account of several million dollars would be tough to lose. They'll pony up more money if you threaten to move the accounts."

The Prince seemed pleased by this initial analysis of his finances. "It's like squeezing an orange," he commented to Jeb. "There are always a few more drops you can get out, yes?" he asked.

"Of course, a good analogy," Jeb answered. "And your portfolio of stocks is way too conservative. They are good if you want to park some money and hold its value, but if you want capital growth, you need to be more aggressive. I can show you…"

"I am sure you can Paul. I am satisfied that you will be a real asset to me. I am like the peasant who is given a tractor. I know how to start it, but little else. You will be my guide."

Jeb was happy that he had met the Prince's expectations. He had some other ideas that he would like to discuss with the Prince, about financing his own bank, for instance. But the Prince's attentions had been drawn elsewhere.

"The time has come for this slave to feel the kiss of a lash," he said as he rose from his chair. Jeb had been sitting on a cushion in front of the Prince and he rose as well.

"I hope you will excuse me your Highness, I want to continue my examination of your financial records," he said. There was no way he intended to witness the savage beating of this helpless girl.

"Absolutely not, Paul. I insist that you stay. If you have never had the pleasure of watching a female dancing to the strokes of a whip, you have not lived." The Prince motioned to the attendant to get him a whip.

Jeb resigned himself to watching the young woman's ordeal. His palms started to sweat and his stomach became tight as he anticipated the harsh treatment that was about to be meted out. He had never seen anyone whipped, not to mention a defenseless girl. He loathed violence. "What kind of man is this Prince?" he thought.

The Prince took possession of a four foot long whip. He stepped over to Vicki and showed it to her. "Do you like it?" he asked her tauntingly. Vicki's eyes swam with tears. She had been anticipating this moment all day, dreading it. She had felt the lash last night, but now her skin had been tenderized, made raw by the heat of the noontime Mediterranean sun. She knew there was no chance that the Prince would renege on his promise to her of the most exquisite pain. If only she could waken from this nightmare!

The Prince approached Vicki, whip in hand. He paused to pinch her ravaged nipples. He pressed his finger to her right breast. The dark pink skin turned white where it had been touched and then reverted to pink. "You see, Paul," the Prince spoke, "you have to let the damage to the skin settle in before it becomes really painful." Vicki moaned as he scraped his fingernails across her breast. "The tits are now ripe. Let's see the ass."

The dangling girl was turned around, revealing a bright pink hue on the twin globes of her behind. It was a sharp contrast to the whiteness of her thighs and back. The Prince gave Vicki's left buttock a hard slap. The girl stiffened in pain and mewed behind her gag. "Yes, the ass is ripe too," the Prince observed. "I think we'll start with the ass. It's not as red as her tits, but we can be a lot harsher there." To the attendant he said, "Strap her thighs together and anchor her feet. I don't want her spinning around avoiding the blows."

The attendant jumped to obey and soon Vicki's legs were joined together and the bracelets around her ankles had been linked and fastened to a "D" ring in the floor. Vicki's body was pulled taut. She could move her hips from side to side, but she could affect little more movement than that. She presented a delectable target for the Prince.

"Here, Paul, rub you hands over her ass. See how hot it is!" the Prince exclaimed.

Jeb reluctantly stepped up and placed his hands on the soon to be agonized flesh. With one hand on each buttock he could feel the heat of the girl's skin. She shifted nervously when she felt his hands press gently against her ass. When Jeb removed his hands, white handprints momentarily flashed. "Her ass really is burned," Jeb thought. "This is going to hurt like hell."

With a nod for Jeb to step aside, the Prince made ready the whip. "She's to get twenty five strokes. Why don't you keep count for me, Jeb?" the Prince asked.

The Prince's request was a command for Jeb. He agreed.

"Whack!" The first blow struck the buttocks, causing the soft flesh to ripple, a streak of white to rise where the lash had landed. The girl jolted her body stiffly and cried out from behind her gag. "One!" called out Jeb.

"Whack!" The second blow fell. The girl stiffened again. Strange sounds came from her throat as her scream of pain was stifled by the bulbous mass that stuffed her mouth. "Two!" Jeb yelled, making sure that his voice could be heard above the violent moans emanating from the poor young girl. Jeb was horrified at what he was witnessing. He could see the glee in the Prince's eyes. "What dark demon drives this man?" Jeb thought. He saw the Prince's arm rise once again.

"Whack!"

"Three," he called.

"Whack!"

"Four!"

And so the beating continued. The poor girl was now thrashing about in her chains, wailing, her body jerking in every direction. But her actions were to no avail as the Prince found his mark every time.

"Whack!"

"Fourteen!"

The ass, which had been bright pink, was now turning a deep red. The sun damaged skin sent wave after wave of pain through the girl's body. Each blow carried an aftermath of hot, burning pain.

"Whack!"

"Fifteen!"

The beating continued. The Prince's brow was dripping in sweat as he put all his effort behind each blow. Now the girl lay limp in her chains. Her voice had become one long moan, rising in volume as each blow was delivered.

"Whack!"

"Nineteen!" Jeb called out. His horror had turned to fascination. There was something about this that paled all other experiences for him. Each moment that the girl struggled and cried out in pain was as intent as a lighted match, almost blinding. To have such power! Jeb's cock had hardened after the first few blows. By now it was a stiff rod of steel. He resisted the urge to stroke it. He felt that the slightest touch would make him come, staining his shorts and his white cotton slacks. He had no idea that it would be like this!

"Whack!"

"Twenty four!"

The Prince paused. He looked at Jeb, grinning. He could see the passion that he had arisen in Jeb. He knew that Jeb would never look at women the same way again. He would measure each one as an object for his pleasure. He would assess each one's tolerance for pain and imagine in his mind her dangling at the end of a chain, awaiting the sting of a forcefully applied whip. The second step in Jeb's corruption had taken place.

"Whack!"

"Twenty five!"

The Prince lowered his arm. Great swaths of sweat circled his armpits. He smiled at Jeb. "Didn't I tell you?" he asked.

Jeb was speechless. The spectacle he had just witnessed was beyond his imagination. Just yesterday, he had been a civilized member of society, obeying its norms, respecting the dignity and rights of others. But here he was, his blood hot, his heart pumping wildly. And before him was a slowly twisting, moaning victim of a brutal assault. Part of him was repelled by what he had seen. Part of him wanted more.

He struggled to find the words to respond to the Prince's interrogatory. What he had just seen and felt could not be put into words. "I, I, I…," he stammered.

The Prince laughed. "Don't speak. You don't have to. I can see for myself."

Jeb stared at the slumped figure before him. Vicki's ass was screaming red. He knew that the pain had to be unbearable. And yet she had to bear it. She had no choice. And there was more to come!

The Prince snapped his fingers and a tray with iced tea appeared. It was placed on the low table where Jeb and the Prince had sat maybe ten minutes before. As he sat down to partake of the much needed refreshment, he knew that he was not the same man he had been when he had stood up.

The Prince also sat. He watched Jeb with a careful eye, appraising the effect of the girl's torment on him. He was a sharp assessor of men's characters. He had to be. And he saw that the pale, young man before him would have no further qualms about the ethics of female slavery.

The men sat silently as they sipped their tea. Vicki's moans and the ever present hum of the ship's engines were the only sounds. The gentle rocking of the boat began to sooth Jeb's passion. He looked at the Prince and found him staring back, peering into his eyes and, perhaps, his soul.

The Prince's gaze then strayed to Vicki's almost lifeless form. She would have to be brought back from her comatose reverie before he began again. His cock too, was hard. There was nothing like a good beating to stir the blood.

Having rested about fifteen or twenty minutes, the Prince stirred again. He downed the remnants of his iced tea and stood. He still had the whip in his hand and contemplated it momentarily. He spoke to the attendant. "Perhaps something lighter for the tits. Get me the number two cane."

Dutifully, the attendant moved towards the cabinet and removed a thin bamboo cane. He handed it to the Prince who appraised it with an expert's eye. Swinging it back and forth, he admired the swishing sound it made in the air. Jeb was up too. Now that his passion had cooled, he had deep misgivings about his reactions to the violent torture of the girl's ass. "Never mind what kind of man he is," he thought, referring to the Prince. "What kind of man am I?"

Without needing instruction, the attendant spun Vicki 180 degrees so that her front was now facing the two men. Jeb could see the redness of the girl's eyes, the pallor of her face. Her demeanor bespoke great torment. The attendant waived something under her nose. She shook her head back and forth, her eyes became alert.

Vicki saw the two men standing before her. Her eyes went to the cane held by the Prince. As she realized that her torment was about to recommence, her brow creased, her nostrils flared.

"And now, the tits," the Prince spoke softly.

Like the girl's ass had been, the twin bulbous globes on Vicki's chest were bright pink, evidence of their harsh treatment by the sun. Jeb stared at them with admiration. He longed to kiss them, to suck on the hard, jutting nipples, to feel their firm heft in his hands.

"After we finish, you can fuck her," the Prince said to Jeb. Jeb just nodded, his prick rising.

Since the cane was thin, it would not do the damage that had been done to Vicki's backside. The breasts were infinitely more tender than the muscles of the buttocks. A lighter, more expert hand was required to straddle the line between torture and damage. The Prince needed these breasts to last so that he could recover his investment. Many men would pay to fondle them, to suck them, to press their cocks between them, and to torment them.

In addition to the pain that Vicki would soon suffer was the humiliation she would feel as her breasts were abused. Nothing marked the visible difference between men and women than the reality of these jutting mounds. Each blow would remind her of her status as an abject victim of the lusts of men. Her breasts were firm, rotund and large. They had many times been the source of pleasure for her as her lovers caressed them, kissed them. When alone, when she was seduced by the need for the self administration of sexual pleasure, she had often used them to heighten her passion, rubbing them, pulling at the nipples, pressing them firmly into her chest.

But now, they were the object of sadistic lust. This man, this self styled prince, intended to abuse them, to strike them with a whip. What had once been the subject of her pleasure, her pride, was now the source of desperate fear.

Behind her, her dark skinned lover knelt. Yolanda's eyes were filled with tears as she viewed the cruel damage that had been done to Vicki's ass. She was too terrified to move, but she yearned to jump to her feet, hold her lover in her arms and with a soft, soothing voice, comfort her. But these hard, ruthless men would inflict the same unspeakable pain on her breasts, her ass, if she as much as shifted her weight. She knelt stock still, as she had been instructed. Her arms ached from being held erect, her hands entwined in her hair to keep her arms from falling.

Her knees ached. Her thighs still stung from this morning's abuse. She could still feel the aftermath of the Prince's cock in her ass, the taste of his cum in her mouth. She was powerless to ease her poor lover's ordeal. She could only exacerbate her own.

"I think that this time we will let the bitch yell and scream," the Prince said. The attendant had anticipated an instruction from the Prince and stepped up to Vicki to remove her gag. He seemed a little confused at first. The Prince had had Demetrius's cheek distending gags placed into the mouths of the two women. The attendant fumbled with the key, and then, getting the hang of it, turned the lock counterclockwise and pulled the gag free.

Vicki seemed disturbed at the removal of the gag. Her mouth twisted in a tortured grimace. She started a little humming sound, a frantic attempt to preserve some of her dignity by delaying the inevitable, desperate pleas for mercy. Her red tinged breasts swung back and forth across her torso as her body shook nervously.

"You know," the Prince commented to Jeb, "a whipping to the breasts is a delicate thing. The object, of course, is pain to the victim. But, if you value the slut, you don't want to damage the muscle tissue. That would cause the breasts to sag and become misshapened. As you can see, I have chosen a thin cane, one that will deliver a quite harsh sting, but will not cause the tearing of any breast tissue."

As he was speaking, the Prince idly patted his palm with the cane. An attendant approached Vicki and began to apply some kind of oil to her breasts. Vicki looked down with dismay, as she knew that anything that was done to her now could only be for the purpose of exacerbating her torment.

"My servant is coating the slut's tits with a spiced oil, the Prince told Jeb. "The oil opens the pores and stimulates the nerve receptacles. This will allow me to ease up on my strokes while magnifying the painful effect of each blow. The result is electrifying."

Vicki, of course, could hear every word that the Prince said. She observed with helpless horror as the attendant slowly rubbed the oil into her breasts. At first, the oil was deceptively soothing to her damaged skin. But then, as the spices took effect, her skin began to burn as the pores opened and the nerve endings on her breasts came alive.

The attendant was enjoying his not solicitous attention to what had been, until now, Vicki's pride and joy. He watched her eyes as they tensed, reflecting the breasts' increase in sensation. Vicki gaze was frozen into his. He smiled.

Tapping the attendant's shoulder with the cane, the Prince signaled him to step aside. Vicki's gaze now focused on the Prince, as she knew that the moment of truth had come. Her face was pathetic as her brow furrowed, her lips became white. She closed her eyes tightly.

The narrow, leather encased cane whistled as the Prince let the first blow strike Vicki's breasts. She jumped at its impact, screeching loudly. "Ahhhhhhhhhhhh!"

"Oh my god, oh my god, oh my god!" she called out. "Ohhhhhhhh!" she moaned. Her eyes were wide open now. She stared at the Prince. "Please, please, please, no more, please!" she exclaimed.

The Prince was remorseless. Smiling, he called out, "One."

He raised he cane again. "Swish, crack!"

Vicki was now without words as her voice rose to a high pitch and a loud, piteous wail escaped her lips. Jeb was overwhelmed at the tableau he was witnessing. The blows to Vicki's ass had been quite different. He did not have to watch her face. Her voice had been stilled. The scene seemed surreal. But it was real. This was really happening.

"Swish, crack!"

"Three!" the Prince called out.

The first blow had struck Vicki's breasts high, above the nipples. The second, being more of an undercut, caught them just below. The third was spot on.

Vicki's voice was now just a continuous wail. She wriggled her hips to and fro, causing her breasts to undulate. Her eyes were clamped shut, her mouth open wide as she tried to voice the horror of the pain she was suffering.

The Prince was methodical in his abuse to the delicate mounds of Vicki's womanhood. Each blow was counted. Each time, Vicki responded with a torrent of cries and a spastic jerk of her body.

Finally, it was done. Vicki's breasts were swollen, violet red. She hung forlornly, sobbing in her chains. Jeb's cock was rock hard, poised to ejaculate. He could think of nothing else but the Prince's promise that he could fuck this suffering wench.

The Prince stepped towards the girl. She was oblivious to his presence until he lightly pinched her nipples. She cringed and drew in her breath. "Are you ready to serve us slave?" he asked her.

Vicki was biting her lip, fighting the urge to cry out. She looked the Prince in the eyes. Here was an opportunity to end her torment. "Yes, yes, I'll do anything," she said softly, hardly daring to speak.

"Release her," the Prince commanded. An attendant raced forward and undid the strap that had held her legs together. Another lowered the chain. Vicki's knees collapsed as she lost its support. The Prince stepped forward and grabbed her arms to prevent her fall. He drew her into his body softly, wrapping his arms around her. He was careful not to crush her tits, but the mere touch of his chest against hers caused her to moan. She was shaking visibly and drooped against the Prince, all of her strength drained.

The Prince gently stroked her hair. Jeb could see, but not hear, that he was speaking softly into her ear. Suddenly Vicki broke down into a torrent of tears. She sobbed uncontrollably encircling the Prince with her arms. Jeb was astounded. Just moments ago the girl was being thrashed within an inch of her life and now she was embracing her tormentor.

The tableau lasted for several minutes. Vicki's sobbing began to subside. The Prince drew her body away from his. "I'm proud of you little one. You bore your whipping well," he told her. Vicki started to cry again and the Prince gently grabbed her neck in his hand and pulled her head up. "Enough of that, now. Enough of that. You promised to serve us, remember?"

Vicki nodded her head.

"Now you are to go with my friend, Paul. He will take you to his cabin and you will give him your body and serve him in any way that he demands. Do you understand?"

The girl nodded again, steeling a glance at Jeb.

"Then you must offer yourself to him. Go and kneel before him."

Vicki hesitated momentarily and then gingerly stepped towards Jeb. Her eyes were downcast, her head bowed. Carefully, she lowered herself to her knees. When she reached the floor, she bent over and placed her palms on the rug. Her ass was raised up slightly, avoiding contact with the back of her legs. Clearly, the girl was endeavoring not to put any pressure on her raw and painful buttocks.

Her almost purple breasts swung below her chest. She was still sniffling, at the very edge of emotional collapse.

The Prince spoke to her again, his voice still soft, but with an edge of insistence. "Vicki, you must beg to be allowed to serve my friend Paul. If he refuses you, that would dishonor me. Your torment is done for now, but remember, tomorrow is another day."

"Yes, y,yes," Vicki stuttered. In a low, mournful voice she spoke to Jeb, "I beg you to let me serve you."

"Now Vicki, you are a slave are you not?" the Prince asked her.

She struggled to hold in her sobs, causing her body to convulse lightly. "Y,yes," she managed to blurt out.

"And what does a slave call the one she serves, Vicki?"

Vicki paused, trying to think of the right answer. She knew that the Prince was unmerciful and cruel. One mistake could cause another round of unbearable torture to begin. She then made the connection. "Master?" she said softly almost as a supplication.

"Yes, Vicki, very good. Now ask Paul again to let you serve him."

Jeb was entranced at the Prince's mental control over this still quite delectable woman. She looked up at him. "Please, may I serve you, master?" she said. Jeb was so taken aback that he hesitated to answer. Vicki began to panic, mistaking his delay for indecision. She intensified her supplications. Her voice a plaintive whine, tears forming in her eyes, she raised her body, proffering her bruised, discolored breasts to Jeb. She renewed her prayer. "I beg to serve you master. Please, please let me serve you. I'll do whatever you say, please?"

Jeb realized that he had witnessed the utter destruction of this woman's personality. A few days ago she had been a carefree, beautiful, young girl, on holiday. Now she was an abject, piteous creature, begging to be raped.

He reached out a hand to touch her head. The touch of her body was electrifying as, in his mind, he pictured her a few minutes before, screaming and dancing to the whip, just as the Prince said she would. His prick was rock hard as he imagined plundering this poor girl's sex. He finally found the words to reply to the trembling slave before him. "Yes, you may serve me."

CHAPTER THREE

Since Carmella's epiphany with Aboud and her eager service of all the men that followed, her life in the bowels of the House of Adeem had changed. Immediately afterwards she had been taken to her bed and allowed to sleep a long time. She woke fully rested for the first time in days. Following her ritual beating that 'morning', and after her shower, she had been taken, not to the refectory, but to another room, one she had not yet visited. She was led there by a matron, a strap affixed to her collar, her hands bound behind her.

When she entered, she saw Aboud standing by a mounted chair in the middle of the room. She was enraptured to see Aboud again. All of her hopes of relief from her daily humiliation and abuse centered on him. He dismissed the matron and grabbed Carmella by the sides of her bald head. He fixed his lips on hers and kissed her deeply. Carmella felt herself melting in his arms. What joy she felt that he had deigned to give her the pleasure of his tongue, his hands, as they ran down her arms and her hips.

She emerged from his kiss breathless. He addressed her. "Slave, today you will be marked with the crest of the House of Adeem. From today you will begin your preparations to serve your master's guests. Learn your lessons well."

He released Carmella from his arms. She saw that they were not alone in the room. A slender, youthful, but mature, woman, dressed not in the drab uniform of the matrons, but in Western clothes, a light green poplin blouse, white cotton pants, stood watching Carmella intently. Her hair was short, but styled. She wore golden earrings, circlets, a gold chain around her neck. She was smiling at Carmella.

"Hello, Carmella," she said. Carmella reveled in the sound of her name. The woman reached out and stroked her gently on her cheek. The delicacy of her touch astounded Carmella. She looked at Aboud, confused, seeking some understanding of this turn of events.

Aboud spoke to her. "This woman will mark you. Obey her." He nodded to the woman and left the room.

The woman's voice had been soft and sweet. Carmella longed to hear it again. Rather than speak, the lithe woman stepped closer to Carmella and removed her leash. She kissed Carmella lightly on the lips. Carmella's eyes began to water. She was grateful to this woman for this moment of warmth and peace. "My name is Jennina, Carmella. I am going to place the mark on you," she said. She caressed Carmella's breast with one hand as she leaned back to get a better look at her. The marks of the many whippings and beatings were all over Carmella's body. She felt ashamed that this woman should see her this way. But the woman did not seem to care. Her eyes flowed over Carmella' body, appreciating it. She reached down and stroked Carmella's belly and then lower, to her sex.

Carmella felt herself opening to the woman's caress. Her consent had not been sought for this graceful, soft, feminine touch, but she would have given it gladly if she had been asked. She leaned her head in the crux of the woman's shoulder as warmth spread through her loins. She began to cry.

"There, there, now Carmella. Let's not be sad. Here, let me mount you in the chair."

Carmella did not want the caress of her pussy to stop, but she obeyed automatically. The woman, Jennina, unfastened the bracelets from behind her back and guided her to the chair. The chair was on a little platform and Carmella had to step up. As she leaned back in the chair, Jennina raised her legs and affixed them to two stirrups affixed to the sides. Carmella felt her legs spread wide. She tried to rise to see what the woman was doing, but she was pushed gently back. A clip was attached at the rear of her collar and her wrists were locked to the arms of the chair.

Carmella began to fret that this tenderness the woman had shown her was merely a prelude to a new form of torment, that her emotions were being played with. Jennina saw the look of worry on Carmella's face.

"Don't be afraid, Carmella," she said. "I'm not going to hurt you." The voice soothed Carmella.

After making sure that Carmella was secured, Jennina stepped away and pulled a little cart and a stool over to the chair. She kept the cart at arms length and sat on the stool between Carmella's legs. Softly, she caressed Carmella's lower belly, the inside of her thighs. She leaned over and kissed the fulcrum of Carmella's slit, lingering over the now hard nub of pleasure. Carmella closed her eyes and drifted into a wave of pleasure.

The woman rose from Carmella's pussy and rubbed her belly. "Here is where the mark will go. You have seen it on the other slaves. It is a sign that you have been deemed worthy to serve your masters. It will mark you forever as a slave of the House of Adeem, a mark of distinction. Anyone who sees it will know that you a skillful and willing creature of pleasure."

Some part of Carmella revolted against what she was being told. Wasn't she once a person? Didn't she once have rights and freedom? What right had they to imprison her and torture her, humiliate and abuse her? But the tender voice of the woman who continued to stroke her sex calmed those stirrings. She longed to be a creature of pleasure. She longed to serve and give her body to others. She knew that this was the only way she could find relief from the whips and chains. To be marked was a blessing she yearned for.

Jennina ceased her ministrations to Carmella's melting crevasse. She took a small pitcher from the cart and poured a tiny cup of a thick, creamy liquid. She brought it to Carmella's lips. "Drink this slave," she said, her voice smooth and sultry, like warm honey.

Carmella happily drank the liquid from the cup. It was slightly bitter, a taste of almonds. It was the most delicious thing that she had had in weeks. She trembled slightly as it flowed down her throat and to her stomach. She felt its warmth spread from her stomach to the rest of her body. Jennina watched her for a few minutes as a cloud of velvet floated through Carmella's brain.

As Carmella drifted into a dream-like state, Jennina began her work. She lowered the back of the chair so that Carmella' stomach was spread taut. She brushed the lower belly with disinfectant. Taking a stencil from a plastic sheath, she spread it out and carefully traced the stencil's design on Carmella's stomach with a thin, black marker. She took a moment to satisfy herself that the design was well placed and clear, and then reached over and turned on the power to a tattoo pen. It took Jennina about an hour and a half to complete her work on Carmella's stomach. Each delicate flourish was added carefully. The flowing "A" at the center of the tattoo was filled with the deep blue ink. Several times, as Carmella stirred, she was given another cup of the soporific.

Finally, the tattoo was complete. The skin was raw and tender where the tattoo pen had bit but Jennina could see that the design had been applied well. She put away her tools and stood up. Carmella was lying languidly in the chair. She had been conscious throughout the application of the tattoo, but her mind floated pleasurably in a foggy sea. The drink had made her slightly euphoric, reinforcing her desire to accept the mark that would set her apart from other women, other slaves. She yearned to be accepted into a sisterhood of pleasure, a sisterhood that she had earned through her torture and torment.

Jennina lowered one of the arms of the chair so that she could step closer to Carmella's body. Softly, she whispered into Carmella's ear, "It is done." She kissed the ear tenderly, running her tongue over its ridges. Carmella let the sensuous warmth of Jennina's tongue flow through her. She felt Jennina's hand on her breast, gently caressing it. The hand cupped the breast, squeezing it softly, a finger delicately stroking the nipple. Through her befogged mind, Carmella could feel a surge of passion arise within her.

Jennina moved her lips from Carmella's ear to her lips. Tenderly she teased the inner ring of Carmella's mouth with her tongue. Her hand had now descended. Arching over the slightly pulsing site of the ornate design that had been applied to Carmella's stomach, it found her pussy, moist with the juices of Carmella's lust. Carmella felt the practiced hand push aside the engorged lips and enter her. She yearned to embrace this tender woman who was so artfully stoking her desire. As she strained to move her arms, Jennina took her lips from Carmella's and softly comforted her with a whispered, "Shhhhh."

Jennina's hand left Carmella's sex, stroking the tender skin on the inside of her thighs. Carmella mewed a sigh of disappointment, but then arched her back as the pleasure of this new sensation coursed through her. Jennina's lips found hers again and sucked gently, coaxing Carmella's tongue from her mouth. Wave after wave of pleasure washed over her. As the hand found her pussy again, as the fingers entered her and found the enthralling point of pleasure within, Carmella began to moan. The hand now grabbed her pussy firmly, administering a driving force that fueled Carmella's need for completion. Her body began to shudder and jerk as she approached the crest of fulfillment. At last the summit was reached and Carmella began to cry out. Jennina drove her tongue deep into Carmella's mouth as Carmella's passion surged. Once over the top, Carmella felt jolt after jolt of almost unbearable pleasure. She bucked and strained at the bindings to her ankles and wrists. She was blinded by delight.

As Carmella reached her surfeit of passion, Jennina slowed her caresses. She squeezed the lips of Carmella's burning sex and then moved her hand again to Carmella's breasts, gently caressing one and then the other. She then circled Carmella's head with her arms and pulled her close, hugging her head, stroking her hair. A gentle warmth now suffused Carmella. She began to sob gently as her gratitude for the gift that Jennina had given her overwhelmed her.

For three days Carmella wore a bandage over her lower stomach, protecting the site of the tattoo. During that time she was kept isolated from the other slaves and free from the random torment that she has suffered before she was marked. Once each day, Jennina came to change the bandage, apply ointment and caress Carmella to orgasm.

On the first day of Carmella's confinement, Jennina appeared with a small disk and a strange instrument in her hand. Spreading Carmella's legs, she took the instrument and applied it to the right side of Carmella's slit. Carmella felt a fierce pain, as a hole was punched through her lower labial lip. Expertly, Jennina clamped a small ring through the hole, a ring which carried a small gold disk. On one side was the crest of the House of Adeem; on the other, Carmella's name.

On the fourth day, Carmella was brought back to the tattoo room and her bandage was removed. Jennina brought out a mirror so that Carmella could see the markings on her flesh. Carmella felt herself transformed by what she saw. The graceful, flowing script, the delicate flourishes that surrounded it, had marked her as a thing of beauty.

Jennina pressed Carmella's shoulders, guiding her gently to her knees. She sat back in the chair where Carmella had sat a few days before. Today, Jennina was wearing a flowing cotton skirt, purple with a yellow border. Her top was a flowered blouse, loose around her neck revealing, invitingly, the tops of her breasts. As she sat down, she raised her skirt exposing her long brown legs and the dark bush at their joinder. Carmella was mesmerized. She had never felt passion for a woman before, but she felt it now. She lusted after that moist, inviting crevasse. But she dared not move without a command. She was a slave. Her wants and desires counted for nothing.

"Slave," Jennina spoke, "pleasure me."

Carmella needed no further encouragement. She rubbed her hands across Jennina's thighs, spreading them and plunged her tongue into the musky odored slit. Jennina uttered a sigh of pleasure as Carmella ran her tongue along the walls of her hot pussy. She stiffened as Carmella sucked gently on the nub of pleasure that surmounted the blood thickened lips. As Jennina's passion mounted, she placed her hands on Carmella's head, gently stroking the nascent growth of hair. Moaning, she reached her climax, shuddering and pressing her thighs against Carmella's head, pushing Carmella's mouth hard against her loins.

When she was finished, she leaned forward and lifted Carmella's head by her chin. She pressed her lips against Carmella's.

Carmella felt proud that she had returned some of the pleasure that Jennina had given her. As Jennina prepared her to reenter the world of the dungeon and her training to come, she was heavy of heart, fearful that she would never see Jennina again. Aside from Aboud, this had been the only source of warmth and safety she had known since the night of her arrest, a night that seemed to have occurred in a far distant past. She thought of Jeb for the first time in many days. She had loved him once. Now he was a mere memory. She had abandoned hopes of ever seeing him again, of ever being held in his arms. She yearned for something to hold on to, some person who she could love and care for.

Jennina joined Carmella's hands behind her back and snapped the leash back onto her collar. She fondled Carmella's breasts gently. "Take care, slave, I will see you again. Train well."

Carmella's heart leapt at the prospect of seeing Jennina again. She would train well, with all of her heart and soul.

Jennina opened the door to the tattoo room and a matron was standing there waiting. She took the leash from Jennina's hand and unceremoniously dragged Carmella through the common room.

"So, did you have fun with the mistress?" she asked harshly. "Did you lick her pussy?"

Carmella hesitated to taint her memory of her time with Jennina, but knew better than to leave a matron's question unanswered. "Yes, madam," she answered in a low voice.

"Well you'll do a good deal of pussylicking from here on in, slave. And I'll bet that you haven't had a good whipping for a while. We'll soon cure that!"

Carmella realized that the idyll of the last few days was over. She was taken to one of the punishment rooms and once inside, she was affixed to a wooden stock, her head captured between its two hemispheres, her hands still locked behind her. The stock was low and she had to bend at the middle to accommodate it. Her legs were fastened together at the ankles. The matron left the room.

She did not know how long she waited for someone to come and administer her beating. She knew that she was being reminded of her status as an abject prisoner. She knew that soon a whip would insult her flesh and that she would yell and moan with pain.

The door opened and someone came into the room. Carmella could not see who it was, nor could she determine whether it was a man or a woman. There was a moment of silence as the unknown person caressed her buttocks and the rear of her thighs, perhaps marking the focus of the whipping to come. Suddenly, Carmella heard the familiar sound of a cane swishing through the air and then felt an intense burning across the back of her thighs. She was determined to absorb the blows without calling out, without any demonstration of the pain she was experiencing. That determination lasted through the fourth stroke of the cane. On the fifth, Carmella moaned loudly. The sixth caused her to cry out. After that she wailed and cried as much as she ever had.

Although Carmella continued to be beaten and abused, there was something different about the way that she was treated after gaining the mark of the House. Some days she avoided all but the obligatory whipping at the beginning of her training day. Her duties changed from being the passive recipient of abuse to that of active engagement in the learning of the skills she would need, and be expected to have, once she was permitted to serve in the rooms above.

Until now, Carmella had not known of the palace of pleasure that existed in the floors above the dungeon. She had not been able to speak to any of her sister slaves and the matrons and trainers had been silent about her future. Even Aboud, who now occasionally took her to his bed and ploughed her body wantonly with his thick, insatiable rod, had never previously said anything about what awaited her after her training.

Now it was self evident, as she was shown how to serve tea gracefully while displaying the charms of her body to the greatest effect. She was given lessons on the many varieties of techniques to pleasure a male organ with her mouth. She even learned a smattering of Arabic, enough to know when to suck a cock, to spread her legs, to make her ass available for the whip or for penetration. Her hair started to grow in, now a fluff of brown on her head. And she was taught how to perform, to dance seductively, to caress herself invitingly.

She had been told that she would have to perform on the platform that stood in the middle of the floor in the dormitory. And she did, either alone, caressing herself to orgasm again and again for the edification of a female audience, or coupled with another young, beautiful, lithe woman, for an exposition in Sapphic love.

The matrons also seemed to change their attitude towards Carmella. She was permitted to eat at the refectory table with the other marked slaves. The interest of the matrons in beating and tormenting her seemed to wane, although there were prominent exceptions to this. But overall, they became more curious about her physical attributes, rubbing and sucking on her breasts, stroking her cunt. And she was made to return the favors. Large, bulbous breasts were forced into her mouth. She was compelled to lick and kiss the sweaty, hairy mass between their thighs.

And of course there were the trainers. Almost every day one of them would select her for their pleasure either in one of the many rooms designed for such use, or in their rooms. She would kneel at the foot of their beds, her collar affixed to the bedpost, awaiting the entrance of her lover for the night. She knew them all by now and knew which ones would torment and abuse her and which ones would give her free reign to pleasure them and be pleasured in return.

Finally, she was told that the next day she would serve in the rooms above. She was kneeling at Aboud's feet, awaiting his pleasure. He had a cane in his hand and was tapping it gently against his palm. "Slave, tomorrow you will serve outside of the training rooms. You have been deemed worthy of serving the Master's guests. Tonight I will mark your breasts and thighs with the cane so that the Master's guests will feel free to abuse you as they see fit. Do not believe that your training is complete. You have much to learn. But if you perform well and give pleasure to the Master's guests you may earn yourself freedom from this dungeon. Now stand so that you may be marked."

Trembling, Carmella rose to her feet. Her hands were bound behind her and she could not, even if she had the foolishness to try, offer any defense to the blows she knew she would soon suffer. But a sense of joy and accomplishment rose in her. She had been deemed worthy!

CHAPTER FOUR

Jeb's voyage through the Mediterranean was drawing to a close. He could see the entrance to the Calipha harbor about three miles ahead. He thought about the last few days and how far he had come.

After Vicki's beating, he had led her down to his cabin with a leash affixed to her collar. She sniffled and cried the whole way. He knew he was going to fuck her, even though it went against every thing he had ever learned. And it wasn't just to stay in character. He wanted to fuck her. He was so turned on by her vicious beating that he was ready to burst.

He opened the cabin door and pulled Vicki in. Magically, a slave girl appeared in the hallway. Not Dina, not the first one, but yet another one. Jeb wondered how many slave girls were aboard the boat. She was a black haired, pale skinned beauty. Her hair was cut in a pageboy with bangs down to just above her eyes. She had a sharp nose and thin lips. Her cheekbones were high, giving her a haughty look. Her breasts hung delicately from her chest with rose red nipples. "Black Irish," Jeb thought.

"May I serve you sir?" she asked.

Her lilting accent told Jeb that he had got it just right. Thinking of Vicki he said, "Yeah, go get some ice and some ointment."

He pulled Vicki inside the cabin and left her standing beside the bed. Her eyes were downcast. Her wheat colored hair hung down her back. Jeb was getting a little tired of her sniveling.

"Shut the fuck up!" he said, more sharply than he intended. The girl scrunched her face muscles tightly and drew a deep breath. Holding it, she was able to bring her sobbing under control.

Within moments, the black haired girl returned. She had a bucket of ice, a tube of ointment and a bottle of 12 year old scotch, single malt, seal unbroken. Jeb was somewhat amazed. "What did they do, pour the unused part of the bottle overboard?"

He told the black haired slave to get some towels from the bathroom. She brought back two hand towels. Jeb wrapped some ice in one and told the slave to gently hold it against Vicki's battered ass. He took the other towel and applied it to her tits.

Vicki gave a sigh of relief as the ice transmitted its coolness to her body. She looked at Jeb gratefully. Jeb just looked away.

They applied the ice for about twenty minutes. Jeb had no desire to know more about this poor girl than he already knew. She was English or British or whatever they called themselves. She was young and beautiful. And, for now, she was his. That's all he wanted to know.

He asked himself why he was bothering to ease this girl's plight when he was going to rape her in a few minutes. Maybe he was just assuaging his guilty conscience? Maybe he still had some residue of compassion left in him? He didn't want to think about it. He did want to think about this desirable creature on her knees with his prick in her mouth.

With the swelling reduced, Vicki had some relief from the consequences of her beating. She was still red and raw though, and so Jeb began to apply the ointment to the damaged portions of her body. He had poured himself a tall scotch and had downed about half of it. He was feeling loose and randy. Rubbing his hands lightly first across her ass, and then gently massaging her breasts, he had felt his cock stiffen. It was time.

Jeb stepped away from Vicki and addressed her. "Are you ready to serve me slave?"

Vicki looked up at him meekly. "Yes master, she whispered.

"I want you to get down on your knees and suck my cock," he told her.

Vicki, with the help of the black haired girl, struggled to her knees. Jeb had quickly disrobed and then sat on the edge of the bed. His legs were spread wide and Vicki moved closer to him. A tear ran down her cheek.

"What the fuck is your problem?" Jeb asked her harshly. She replied in a small, tortured voice.

"I've never done this before, master. I'm afraid that if I don't do it right you'll beat me." She started sniffling again.

Jeb thrilled at the idea that he would be the first to discharge his come in this girl's mouth. At the same time, he sympathized with her fears.

"Just take my cock in your mouth and caress it with your tongue and lips. I'll tell you what to do."

Tentatively, Vicki bent down, her head at Jeb's waist, and meekly took his already stiff cock into her mouth. At first she just held it there, overwhelmed by the unusual experience of a hot, pulsing organ in her mouth. No doubt the taste was slightly salty as she absorbed the sheen of sweat that had built up there. Jeb became impatient.

"Start sucking!" he commanded. "Suck on it and move your head up and down."

The girl tightened her grip on his cock with her lips and began to suck gently. She slowly moved her head up and down, causing Jeb to moan with pleasure. Meanwhile, unbidden, the dark haired girl had crawled onto the bed and placed her body behind Jeb's. She pressed her tits into his back and began to caress his chest. Jeb had never had two women at once, and the delights inherent in it became immediately apparent to him.

Vicki continued her patient oral ministration to Jeb's cock. She was getting the hang of it, being rewarded with a moan or shudder from Jeb when she had done it just right. Jeb felt his blood rise and encouraged Vicki to get on with it. "Faster, harder," he gasped.

Placing his hand in her hair, he began to guide her mouth up and down on his prick. Vicki made some small sounds as she was overwhelmed by the forcefulness of Jeb's hand.

"Move your tongue around, lick it, lick it!" Jeb exhorted her.

Gradually, the surge of Jeb's passion began to force a climax. He bucked his hips as he ruthlessly pushed Vicki's head up and down. The Irish girl was rubbing her tits against his back, caressing his stomach, kissing his neck. Ultimately, he could withhold his climax no longer and he began to ejaculate into Vicki's mouth.

The heretofore unexperienced sensation of a throbbing dick in her mouth startled Vicki. She tried to pull away, but Jeb held her head firmly against his loins. His hot semen shot into her mouth and slowly dripped down her throat. Vicki experienced the bitter salty taste of a man's discharge for the first, but certainly not the last time.

Jeb felt momentarily sated. Holding Vicki's head to his loins, he took in the view of her bruised and still swollen ass. It was amazing to Jeb to be able to appreciate the hideous beauty in the discolorations of Vicki's skin. Bright purple swirls, mixed with reds and pinks. A tapestry of violent passion.

Temporarily physically sated, Jeb mentally wanted more. He wanted to fuck her and was determined to do it. He needed to regroup he forces, and so he pushed Vicki away and stood up. A shower would reinvigorate him. Pouring himself another three fingers of malt, he told the Irish slave girl, "I'm going to take a shower. Make sure that she is ready for me when I come out."

"As the gentleman commands," replied the pale beauty.

Jeb stepped into the shower and let the hot water run over him. His mind wandered through the events of the last twenty four hours. He had lived as intently as he had ever done. Besides the heights of pleasure and passion he had experienced, there was the fact that he was living on a razor's edge. His whole life, it seemed, had been a high wire act, preparing him for just these circumstances. Life was coming at him like a roaring train. He loved it.

When he returned to the bedroom, he was presented with an unexpected spectacle. He had wondered what the long sashes around the waists of the slaves were for, and now he knew. Vicki was lying on her back on the bed, her arms still affixed behind her. Her legs were upraised, pulled up almost to her shoulders. The Irish lass had tied the ends of the cords around Vicki's ankles and run it through the back of her collar. She was splayed open, her bruised breasts at rest. The black haired girl had been tonguing Vicki's slit. She arose, smiling, and said, "She is ready for your use, sir."

She was indeed. Just the sight of her made Jeb's cock tingle. Vicki was obviously in the throws of passion. Her breath was labored, her chest almost as red as her tits. Liquid dripped from her pussy, which was spread wide like an opening flower. Jeb had given a command and it had been obeyed. As he knelt on the bed, the dark haired beauty began to stroke his thighs. She delicately caressed his cock, bringing it to full hardness.

Jeb wasted no time in mounting the grotesquely displayed woman. He pressed his cock against her hot, juicy cunt and entered it. Vicki sighed as she was filled with his hot meat. Her eyes were rolled back into her head, her mouth was open. Jeb slowly pressed his cock deep inside her until his hips met hers. He then slowly retreated, drawing a low moan from the blond girl.

The other girl did not remain idle. Caressing Jeb's buttocks, she gently pushed aside the cheeks of his ass and began to tongue the puckered star between them. Now it was Jeb's turn to feel a new sensation. The feeling of the black haired girl's tongue at the entry of and then deep within his anus was electric. His thighs slapped against Vicki's ass and her moans of pleasure mixed with those of pain. Her tits rocked with the force of his exertions and he could not resist placing his lips on the bruised and damaged nipples. Vicki moaned in pain as he sucked them violently.

Jeb had never been so impassioned in his life. A portal opened in his mind and he passed into a dark place, a place where he could not imagine living without the freedom to exploit the bodies of women as he pleased. He leaned forwards and pressed his body into Vicki's crushing her tormented breasts. When he came, he groaned loudly, his body stiffened, overwhelmed by the intense pleasure of his release. Vicki came too, moaning and crying out, her hips thrusting against his.

The next few days passed for Jeb as if in a dream. Each night he was brought to new levels of delight as he ravaged either Vicki or her brown skinned lover, accompanied by, and with the assistance of one of the Prince's well trained slave girls. While Vicki was taut and shy, Yolanda was luxurious and brazen. It seemed that a whole new world had opened for her. The Prince had encouraged Jeb to experience the pleasure of using Yolanda's ass, and she responded to his invasion of her rear opening with powerful orgasms.

During the days, the two lesbians would entertain the two men, lapping at each other's slits, kissing, smothering each other's breasts with their lips. Only Yolanda had suffered another beating. Her wails and cries excited Jeb to no end.

Finally, the ship made port and coasted to a graceful stop at a crowded pier in Calipha Bay. The ship became a torrent of activity as the sailors and servants scurried about, making ready for the Prince and his Royal guest to go ashore. Standing near the gangway, Jeb watched as twelve burkha clad women, each connected by a chain that ran from the back of their neck to the front of the one behind, tiptoed down the ramp. Jeb had wondered how many slave women were aboard, and now he knew.

Rashid appeared with Vicki and Yolanda in tow. He had hold of their hands on either side of them and appeared to be tugging them forward. Jeb was surprised to see them dressed in their bikinis.

When they were brought to the side of the Prince, he spoke to them.

"You have pleased me well. I have decided to release you."

The girls looked at each other with wonderment. Before they could speak their obvious joy, the Prince continued.

"The British consulate is three blocks inland. If you go there, they will make arrangements to take you back to England."

The girls looked ashore uncertainly. Rashid released their hands and, seeing that they were really free, they rushed down the ramp towards freedom. They made it about 100 yards from the ship when Jeb saw them stopped by a pair of uniformed men. A police car was parked nearby, its lights flashing. Jeb could see that the girls were speaking to the officers. Vicki raised her hand and pointed towards the yacht. Suddenly she was spun around and one of the policemen grabbed her arms and joined them together at the wrists. Yolanda tried to pull away, but was quickly subdued and her hands were then joined behind her back. The two girls were placed in the police car and it sped away.

Jeb was taken aback at what he had just witnessed. He looked over at the Prince, who was smiling wryly.

"You know, Paul, we are a very conservative society. It is a great crime for a woman to display her body in public. And to have entered our country without proper documents, well, that too is a crime. Only spies would do such a thing."

"You mean," Jeb asked, astounded, "they have been arrested?"

"Of course," replied the Prince. "They will be tried fairly and, I'm sure, receive harsh sentences."

"And will we see them again?"

The Prince clapped a hand on Jeb's shoulder. "If you wish it," he said.

Jeb contemplated the future ravishment of the now certainly forlorn women.

A thought came to him. "Prince?"

"Yes, Paul."

"I've been wondering. The marks that your slave girls carry on their stomachs, what does it mean?"

"You mean the tattoos? Well, that is my mark of ownership. The scriptive "A" represents my family name, my middle name, Adeem. Harim Adeem Baroof."

CHAPTER FIVE

Carmella had been told that she was worthy to serve the Master's guests. She had been told so by Aboud, her trainer, in the sequestered atmosphere of his personal bedroom in the dungeon below the public portion of the whorehouse known as the House of Adeem. Aboud had beaten her that night, as was only proper, to remind her of her lowly status and to reinforce her duty as an enslaved object of pleasure.

But that night, it was Aboud who had supplied the pleasure. After he had meticulously delivered ten strong strokes of the cane to her breasts and thighs, he had taken her in his arms and kissed her. She welcomed his hot tongue in her mouth as the burning kisses of the cane still reverberated on her body. Her loins burned with desire for him, she yearned to enwrap his thick, heavy cock with her lips.

Aboud released Carmella's wrists from the chain that had held them over her head. He gently swept her legs from under her and carried her to his lush, four-posted bed. Laying her down, he placed his naked, finely sculpted body next to hers. Carmella was in a trance. Throughout all of her torments during her training, Aboud had been, with one exception, her sole source of comfort and hope. To say that she loved him would do an injustice to the strength of her feelings. She adored him, as a creature would adore its god.

Carmella was enthralled as she felt the heat of Aboud's flesh. She awaited only his command to apply all of her impassioned skills to his pleasure. But he was the master. She knew that she must await his command since what she wanted, what she desired, meant nothing. She was only a slave.

Aboud drew Carmella's hands above her head and locked them in the grasp of his powerful right hand. With his left, he caressed Carmella along the length of her body.

The room was lit only by a small lamp that stood beside the bed. The dim light created a dream like atmosphere. Aboud took Carmella's breast in his mouth and delicately bit down on the nipple. His left hand caressed her stomach and then found the hot, wet crevasse between her thighs. Carmella moaned, spreading her legs wide to grant Aboud the access he desired. Gently, slowly, he caressed her burning pussy. He pinched the small, hard nipple at its apex, first softly, then slowly increasing the pressure until Carmella, arching her back, sighed deeply, "Ohhhhhhhhhhhhhhhh!"

Releasing the sensitive bud, Aboud thrust three fingers deep into Carmella' reverberating canal. Carmella's lower lips were flush and loose, her interior tight and hot. Her breath came shorter and shorter as Aboud urged her to her climax. He began to rub Carmella's clit with his thumb and bit down hard on her breast. As a wave of passion spread over her, prelude to her climax, Carmella's body began to rock and pulse. When she could no longer hold back, she cried out, "Ah, ah, ah, ah, ahhhhhhh!"

Three times Aboud drove Carmella to the height of passion using only his mouth or his hands. Although his cock demanded relief, Aboud was a disciplined man and concentrated on his goal. This slave was something special to him. He had trained more than a hundred slaves for the

Prince's house of delight. He had fucked and whipped a hundred more. They meant nothing to him, mere beasts of pleasure. Somehow, he had experienced a form of human spark in Carmella that he had not found before in any other of the fine and delectable young women who had been ruthlessly torn from their former lives and had found their way to these dungeons. So tonight, he was determined to bind her to him closer than any other slave that had come before.

Binding to their trainers was an expected and planned result of the regimen spelled out for the training of female slaves at the House of Adeem. After all, no one could live long without some hope of human contact. The newly broken slave needed something to fix on, some reason to endure the many torments that she was subjected to. Once the slave had made the commitment of true bondage to the trainer, it was easy to transfer that commitment to service of all the clients, both male and female, who would thereafter stand in the trainer's place. Each client who used her would wear the trainer's face. Each command would be in her trainer's voice. Each sigh of pleasure would emanate from his lips. The slave would devote the same intense, unreserved commitment to the client's pleasure as they would to her master and overlord.

But Aboud's actions were beyond the pale, a terrible deviation from the well tested and proven protocols of the House of Adeem. The commencement of a slave's service in the public areas of the House should mark a point of diminished contact between the slave and her trainer. Aboud should have been testing her training this night, using her ruthlessly and driving her to extremes of obedience and subservience, establishing a distance between himself and the slave. But his devotion to Carmella's pleasure was calculated by him to have the opposite effect.

Carmella was delirious. Aboud was an expert manipulator of women's physical passions and he had used all of his experience and skills on her, pushing her beyond where she had ever been. She moaned and cried out repeatedly as her fevered passion grew. Finally, Aboud mounted the slave. He pushed his thick, hard cock past her plush labial lips, lips that were electrified with sensation. Carmella gasped as she felt the tool of the god that she adored enter her. All of her mind was focused on the slithering passage of Aboud's taut, hot cock inside her. She wrapped her legs around his back, desperately trying to drive him deeper. When he discharged his hot fluids into her womb, his cock pulsing, his hips thrust hard against hers, she also achieved release, calling out his name, begging him to fill her, to possess her.

Aboud awoke several hours later, Carmella wrapped in his arms. He knew that he had done wrong. What good would it do this slave to continue to yearn for him? Aboud knew the hazards that awaited Carmella in her services above ground. She would be available to anyone who desired her. Men would whip her, beat her, fuck her in the most callous and degrading fashions, demand scurrilous services from her. She did not belong to him, she belonged to the Prince.

While in training, Carmella had been in the hands of experts in the training and disciplining of slaves. They knew how far they could drive a slave, how to inflict pain almost scientifically. To them, a captive female was the raw material of a creature of pleasure, a personality to be molded. They would no more damage her than would a shepherd harm a beast in his care.

The clients, however, had no such reservations. While inflicting death on a slave was forbidden, virtually all else was allowed. Damage to a slave became merely an invoice item, a service charge to a membership fee. Aboud and his fellow trainers, and even the cruel, sadistic matrons, were dispassionately applying a regimen of pain and humiliation designed to produce a creature totally dedicated to the service of others. The clients' sole concern was their own passions, and often in their exhilaration went beyond their intentions. Only in the House of Adeem did they have the freedom to abandon themselves to their deepest, darkest desires,

So, while Carmella perceived her promotion, as it were, to the precincts that lay above ground as a liberation from her remorseless oppression, Aboud knew that that world above was full of danger and mindless cruelty.

The next morning, Aboud hustled Carmella from his room. She was bathed and breakfasted in the normal manner. The attending matron led her to the preparation room. It was here that Carmella would be dressed and decorated for her first day of service. She was adorned in a long, turquoise, chintz skirt that flowed around her when she walked. The tips of her breasts and her lower lips were rouged, her face made up. A sweet, delicate perfume was applied to her body. As she was led to the wrought iron gate that barred the stairs to the upper rooms, a matron gave her final instructions. She was one of the training matrons, and she had helped teach Carmella the fine art of graceful service, how to pour a man's drink, bent over, displaying her naked and inviting breasts. She was taught how to walk seductively, her hips swaying slightly. She was taught to arch her back when being examined, to stand so that the lips of her pussy were always visible. All male guests were to be called "sir", a woman "madame". But most importantly, she was taught to open herself at command, to use her crevasse to squeeze the male member, to give oral delight. And when she was to be whipped, to obey, acquiesce in and facilitate her own abuse.

Newly trained slaves were used in the common areas. Later, when she had proven herself, she would be made available to the guests for use in the private rooms. Carmella was led to her first 'posting' barefoot and blindfolded, with her wrists bound behind her. A leash had been clipped to the ring in the front of her slave collar and she followed its lead blindly. Somehow, the fact of being partially clad, the loose skirt flowing as she walked, made her feel more naked above. She could feel her breasts sway as she was tugged quickly through unknown corridors by unseen hands. She marveled at the feel of the cool marble beneath her feet. Her ears perked to hear the sounds of this new world. She heard voices, the sharp click of high-heeled shoes. She sensed the presence of others as she passed them in the hallways.

Carmella's duty station this day was a small lounge. When her blindfold was removed, she saw a brightly lit room, the sun pouring in through large, tinted windows. There were five cloth covered easy chairs in the room, each bright blue. Several large ottomans were scattered about, ominously bedecked with gold plated rings at the corners and sides. A large column stood at the far end of the room, a chain dangling from near its top. The ceiling was high and the walls were covered by textured wallpaper with large blue and yellow flowers. The rug was plush, in an oriental style, with patterns of colors that blended with the walls and chairs.

Carmella had forgotten that such luxury existed. The soft weave of the rug felt like a caress to her feet. And to see the sun!

She had been led to the lounge by a small, brown skinned, Asian man. After he removed her blindfold and freed her wrists, he looked at Carmella dispassionately as he explained to her where the refreshments were kept, on a long console along the wall opposite the windows. He instructed her to kneel, her arms behind her, her knees apart, until such time as a guest gave her a command.

Carmella waited nervously, alone in the elegantly appointed room. To be alone and unfettered was a new experience for her. All during her training, she had either been under the watchful eye of a trainer or a matron, or had been affixed in some way, locked to a ring in the wall or floor, or bound with her hands behind her back.

She stared out the large windows that lined the outer wall of the room, awed by the panoramic view. That was the world out there, a sand and rock strewn wasteland under a tortuous sun. She had the sudden urge to run to the window and somehow smash through it in a bid for freedom. But where would she go? How could she hide from the inevitable pursuers? And, if she did evade capture, how long would a seminude, barefooted woman last in the unrelenting heat of the desert? But that was exactly why she could be left alone in this room. Escape was a mere fantasy.

It was about twenty minutes later that the door to the room opened and two young, European men walked in. One was a heavyset man, with black hair and a rough, unshaven face. The other was slighter in build, clean shaven with long, curly, light brown hair. They took no notice of Carmella as they strolled over to two chairs by the windows. As they sat, the slighter man looked over to Carmella and motioned her to approach.

The men were speaking animatedly, presumably continuing a heated debate that had begun some time before. They were not speaking English, but rather some Slavic or other Eastern European tongue. As Carmella timidly approached them it occurred to her that these men were from the outer world. After today, or tomorrow, they would be returning to a civilized place, where there were women who were not slaves, who did not wantonly display their breasts to unknown men, did not advertise their complete sexual availability through translucent clothing. These men knew, but did not care, that she had been unwillingly plucked from some other life and condemned to a life of abject servitude. If nothing else, the bracelets and collar that she still wore advertised her as a prisoner to be used as their whims took them.

The slight man turned absent mindedly to Carmella and in heavily accented English ordered her to bring two glasses of cold white wine. Hard spirits were forbidden in the House of Adeem. For one thing, drunkenness obscured the experience of pleasure that was the House's trademark. Secondly, it too often led to the kind of lapse in judgment that resulted in the premature obsolescence of slaves.

Carmella murmured quietly, "As the gentlemen wish," and walked as graciously as her anxiety permitted over to the console to retrieve the requested beverages from a golden hued bottle which lay in a bucket of ice. She returned with two partly filled glasses on a small tray. As she proffered the glasses to the men, she leaned over so that her breasts swayed away from her body. Casually, the smaller man reached out and stroked her nipple. The men took the glasses and returned to their debate.

Returning to her original station, Carmella sank back to her knees and placed her hands behind her back. Her heart was beating wildly, knowing that any moment she could be called to perform her real task, the service of their sexual pleasure.

The men continued their excited discussion, heedless of Carmella's presence. The door opened again and all eyes moved towards it. A thin, grey haired man entered. He was somewhat frail and sported a long, grey handlebar moustache. His skin was a light tan, bespeaking a Middle Eastern origin. He was dressed casually, in a loose, colorful patterned shirt, buttoned at the neck, and dark blue cotton pants. The two East Europeans returned to their discussion. The man paused halfway into the room and took a long appreciative look at Carmella. Despite the fact that Carmella had remained naked and exposed for more than two months, open to the cold examination of all, she was disconcerted by the gaze of this wizened man. Perhaps it was his age, old enough to be her grandfather, or perhaps it was the gleeful expression he donned while taking in her charms. In any case, and to her own amazement, Carmella blushed.

The man spoke to her. "What a lovely sight! Please, dear child, bring me an iced tea and then let me caress your breasts."

Carmella was taken aback by the combination of sweetness and brazenness of the old man's request. She had fantasized about what her first sexual encounter as a whore would be, but this was not what she had imagined. While the man found himself a chair, Carmella obeyed his command. She brought him a brimming glass on her small tray. Her breasts quivered as she leaned over to present them and the drink to him.

He received the glass and took a long swig. Carmella placed her tray on the floor and proffered him her breasts. The man placed the glass on a small table next to the chair and laid his hands on the pale, delicate mounds. Surprisingly, his touch was soft, gentle. He pulled Carmella closer and placed his lips on her right nipple. She felt the familiar warmth rise in her loins as he softly sucked on her teat. He shifted to the left breast, and Carmella's other nipple hardened obediently.

She was oddly embarrassed to have her breasts caressed by this old man's mouth as the two other men chatted on obliviously. "So this is what it is like to be a whore," she thought.

The loving treatment of her breasts caused Carmella's pussy to moisten and dilate. She closed her eyes and blocked out all else besides the warmth of the man's lips.

He rose from his oral appreciation of Carmella's teats. "You have wonderful breasts my dear. Tell me your name."

Softly, Carmella said her name.

"Ah, Carmella, you are surely a treasure. Bring that ottoman over and lie on your back."

Carmella complied. When she lay down in front of him, she spread her skirt open so that he could have access to her sex. The light, revealing skirt was split in the front and the back so that her sex and rear were readily available for use. Carmella parted the skirt and spread her legs, anticipating her first customer's desire.

"No, No, bring the ottoman closer," the old man instructed her. "Give me your legs."

Carmella shifted the ottoman so that it almost touched the man's knees and raised her legs, placing them on the arms of the man's chair. He tenderly stroked the length of her thighs cooing softly. His hands were strong, but soft, and Carmella languidly accepted the calming caresses. Then, pulling Carmella closer to him, he began to softly massage the fleshy mound in between. Carmella could feel herself moistening as his thumb entered her. The wizened, yet gentle, man continued his faint cooing sounds as if he were comforting a child. The sounds of his deep voice lulled Carmella and she felt as if having this man caress her sex while she lay splayed before him was the most natural thing in the world.

He placed his hands behind her knees, and he raised her higher so that her buttocks were resting in his lap, her ankles on his shoulders. He bent over and ran his tongue the length of the moist divide between her labia. Carmella shivered with pleasure.

Slowly, expertly, the old man stimulated her with his lips and his tongue. Each time she approached orgasm, he slowed, letting her fires cool before recommencing his oral assault. Carmella's breath came in short spasms as the power of her excitement began to overwhelm her. It went on for more than ten minutes, more like fifteen. Finally, he let her come, and she moaned and cried out in her passion.

"You have a luscious cunt, Carmella," he whispered to her.

Carmella, her chest still heaving from her exertions, anticipated a command to take him in her mouth, or to have her reposition herself so that he could ravish her with his cock. But the man continued to ministrate to her pussy and thighs, stroking them with his hands. When he was satisfied that she had cooled from her passionate release, he leaned over and again placed his mouth on her crevasse.

This time he kept Carmella longer near the brink of coming. Just when Carmella began to shake and quiver in anticipation of another crises, he would change rhythm, alter his caress. Carmella was kept in a state of high excitement for more than twenty minutes. She longed to beg for release, but knew that to speak out, even in passion, would be wrong. In the midst of her almost painful delight, Carmella noticed that the other men had stopped speaking, diverted from their conversation by her groans of pleasure. She sensed their eyes on her and her ordeal. Her momentary distraction ended as the old man took her clit in his teeth and bit down teasingly. She could no longer control her responses as she began to shiver and shake, crying out loudly.

Fluid gushed from Carmella's sweet divide as she experienced her second orgasm. Her thighs quivered, her eyes rolled back. Her hands rubbed at her stomach, aching to caress her breasts. But even in her semiconscious delirium she remembered her training. She had no right to touch herself, to caress her own breasts. She squeezed her hands into small fists as wave after wave of pleasure rode through her.

When her second orgasm subsided, the grey haired man released her legs, grabbed her arms and pulled her up onto his lap. She could smell her juices on the man's face. He kissed the tips of her breasts. "Ah, Carmella," he said, "if only I were ten years younger!"

The other two men had risen from their seats. The heavyset one had removed his rigid cock from his pants and was stroking it slowly. The other man spoke. "If you're finished…."

"Oh, yes," he said. "Please, take her, with my complements."

He pushed her from his lap and her arm was grabbed by the heavyset man. He took hold of her breast and squeezed it hard, making Carmella wince. The slighter man pulled the ottoman away from the chair and Carmella was pushed face down on it. She could hear the soft hiss of clothes being removed.

Carmella felt her ass cheeks being spread and the pressure of a steel hard cock at the entrance to her bowels. She had not had time to prepare herself, to loosen her muscles so as to ease the man's entrance. The heavy man uncaringly pressed his prick past the wrinkled access. Carmella squirmed and whined as her dry, tight anal opening was split wide. Her ass burned as the man's thick, hard cock forced its way.

She was facing the heavy set man's companion and he pulled her head up by her hair and jammed his cock into her mouth. Literally moments ago, Carmella had been writhing to the pleasurable ministrations of the grandfatherly man's tongue. Now she was rudely plugged fore and aft, subject to the pounding thrusts of the two younger men.

She was unable to regulate her assault. She had been trained to focus her skills on the bodies that possessed her, but her rough handling by the two men precluded any application of her learned techniques. The men pressed their cocks home ruthlessly. Carmella, in all her time in training had never felt so meanly used. This was nothing but a callous rape, a remorseless use of her mouth and ass.

The men grunted their pleasure as they rammed Carmella unmercifully. It was not long before Carmella was pumped full of their viscous spunk. As the cock in her mouth spilled its seed down her throat, she was filled with the discharge of the thick, hard prick in her rear.

The men left her lying face down on the ottoman as they dressed themselves. Carmella had gone from the height of bliss to utter debasement. Her ass burned, her jaw ached. She did not move as she heard the two men leaving, jesting with each other. When she looked up, the old man had gone.

The lounge filled up and emptied several times before her shift ended. She was rogered many times, fore and aft, and her mouth was used as well. When able, Carmella retreated to a small water closet and washed her loins and rear in the bidet and wiped away the oozing, white liquids that ran down her thighs. She rinsed her mouth to make it fresh, readying herself for reuse.

Finally, another dark skinned, diminutive servant came to fetch her. Her hands were rebound behind her and she was again blindfolded. Led from the room by a leash, she stumbled along as she traversed the cold marble floors.

CHAPTER SIX

The next day Carmella was returned to the lounge. This time, when her blindfold was removed, there was another slave already there. She was on her knees servicing a large, fat man, his belly rolling over the top of his trousers. There were two other men there, sitting separately from each other. One was reading a newspaper; the other was engrossed in the oral attentions that the pretty, youthful slave was giving to the fat man's cock. He immediately called Carmella over and she fell to her knees before him. At his command she withdrew his erect manhood from his pants and began to suck its tip.

She did not notice when the large East European who had abused her the day before entered the room. She was absorbed in her task, slowly moving her lips up and down on the hard flesh. She circled the tip with her tongue and then plunged down again, absorbing the man's cock down to his stomach, pushing it down into her throat. She was gratified when the man began to moan and the thick meat in her mouth began to throb. She swallowed his salty discharge and withdrew only when she felt his penis soften.

The blond girl was kneeling by the credenza that held the refreshments. Carmella was about to join her there when her arm was grabbed by the man from the day before. She had not recognized him as she walked past his chair. She was startled when she saw who it was.

"Yes, cunt," he said. "It's me. I'm back for some more fun."

Carmella did not know how to respond. She had the urge to flee, but knew that flight would be useless. She sensed the deep cruelty of the man and she knew that she had much to fear from him. His grip was like a vice, sending a shooting pain up her arm into her shoulder. Hoping that she could deflect his cruelty with meekness, she answered the man in a small, self-effacing voice.

"If it pleases the gentleman," she said.

"Oh, it pleases me," he answered in his heavily accented English.

The man she had just serviced spoke to him. "Take it easy on her, Sergi, she's a good little whore." He had a hint of amusement in his voice.

"But good little whores are meant to be beaten," Sergi replied.

Carmella quailed at Sergi's observation. Sergi rose from his seat and grabbed Carmella's breasts. He squeezed the nipples hard, causing Carmella to moan. He was at least a foot and a half taller than her and he began to pull Carmella's nipples upwards, stretching her breasts. She tried to assuage the pain by standing on her tiptoes, but Sergi kept raising her nipples higher and higher.

"This good little whore has nice tits," Sergi said to no one in particular. "I'll bet she would like them stroked with a cane. Wouldn't you, slut?" he asked Carmella.

Carmella was having difficulty holding in a cry of pain. She strained to answer him. "As it pleases the gentleman," she managed to say, although her high pitched voice betrayed her pain and fear.

"I'm no fucking gentleman, cunt," Sergi replied. "I'm going to make you remember me."

He pulled Carmella by the nipples over to the column that sported the dangling chain. Still holding her nipples, Sergi gave Carmella a command, "Take off your skirt!"

It was difficult for Carmella to comply while standing on her toes, but she was able to slide the waistband of the pale yellow skirt past her hips. She strained to push it further down, panicked that this man would become enraged if she failed to obey him, no matter how impossible the task. Finally she was able to slide the waistband down her thighs. By wriggling her hips she was able to get the skirt to slide down her legs to the floor.

Carmella felt proud of the privilege to wear a skirt, even one as thin and sheer as this one. It also seemed a kind of protection. It was a badge of her good training, her skills as a whore. "Who would beat a woman who could give them such pleasure," she had thought. But now she realized that being pretty, compliant and skilled at the arts of love were no assurance that she would not suffer.

Sergi kicked the skirt aside. Give me your wrists, cunt," he said as he finally released Carmella's nipples. Reluctantly, Carmella complied. Sergi grabbed one end of the chain and affixed it to the bands of her wrist bracelets. It passed through a ring on the ceiling and descended to a hook on the column. Sergi pulled it tight, raising Carmella's arms above her head until she was again on her toes.

After securing the chain to the column, Sergi re-addressed himself to Carmella's breasts. He squeezed the nipples again, hard, and then began slapping them viciously, back and forth. His large hands stung Carmella's breasts as he alternated hitting her with his left hand and his right. Each blow dragged a whimper of pain out of her mouth. As the skin began to redden, the stinging became more intense. Smiling, Sergi methodically continued his assault seeing that his efforts were bearing fruit. Carmella could not withhold little cries of pain as the slapping got harder and harder.

All eyes in the room were on the spectacle of Carmella being abused. Even the blond slave was taken aback by the intensity with which Sergi was beating her. She knew that soon the men would be aroused and would seek out her body as a receptacle for their lusts. She would, of course, do anything that they wished, but she was especially motivated to escape the attention of this madman, Sergi.

Sergi interrupted his slapping of Carmella's breasts to again take hold of her nipples and squeeze them between his thumb and forefinger. He twisted them painfully, as Carmella grimaced in agony. Her breasts were hot and had turned a deep pink. Sergi examined them closely, fondling them in his hands. "Yes, these tits are almost ready for the cane," he said. "A little more redness, perhaps."

The bulky man walked over to the credenza where he opened a cabinet. He pulled out a small instrument. As he returned to Carmella, she saw that it was a block of wood with sandpaper affixed.

"Ever have your tits sanded, cunt?" Sergi asked Carmella.

Carmella was so frightened by the prospect that she failed to answer. "Crack!" Sergi slapped her across the face. "Crack!" he slapped her with the other hand. Carmella cried out in pain.

"When I ask you a question, cunt, you will answer it! Do you understand?" yelled the red faced man. Carmella nodded fearfully. "We'll try it again. Ever have your tits sanded, cunt?"

"N,no sir," Carmella managed to squeak out.

"Well, it makes them good and raw. They'll be raw for days. And I'll be back each day to torment them. Would you like that, bitch?" Sergi was inches away from Carmella's face. She could feel his sour, hot breath.

"What have I done to deserve this?" she thought. She trembled at the idea of day after day of torment from this man. Tears flowed down her cheeks. She had been trained to obey the harshest command, to remain meek and passive in deference to a guest's wishes. But here it was, her second day of service as a whore, and she was being tortured unmercifully. She had seventeen years to serve as a slave. How would she ever live through them?

She knew that failure to answer this taunting question would be grounds for further abuse. She had been taught many rote phrases during her training. She now uttered one. "As you please, sir," she said, her voice cracking with fear.

Sergi grinned. "Yes, as I please. And it pleases me to watch you suffer." He began to rub Carmella's breasts with the fine-grained sand paper. It was light enough to irritate and scour the skin, but not rough enough to tear it away. The scratching of the paper set Carmella's breasts on fire. Carefully, holding her body close to his with his arm wrapped around her back, he sanded all around the circumference of each breast. He took his time, meticulously scraping the top layer of skin on every square inch as Carmella whined and moaned. Her breasts were becoming raw and angrily red and yet the man continued her torture. As he abraded her nipples, Carmella's moans of pain became cries. Her knees weakened and she dangled helplessly.

When he was done with the sandpaper, Sergi stepped back and admired his work. The breasts were a bright red, contrasting sharply with the pale white skin of Carmella's chest and stomach. Sergi flicked his finger at one of Carmella's nipples. She jumped in pain, letting out a baleful cry.

"Yes," Sergi said. "You're ready."

He went back to the cabinet and put the sanding block away. He returned with a thick, long gag. He brought it over to Carmella. "Now, we don't want our fun disturbed by a lot of noise, do we?"

Carmella, her face awash with tears, trembling with fear, whispered, "No, sir."

She opened her mouth wide as Sergi jammed the gag in. It filled her mouth back to her throat and forced her teeth apart. Sergi buckled it behind her head. Carmella was almost glad that he had gagged her. She knew that when the cane began to fly, she would beg and plead to be spared. Now, at least, she would avoid that debasement.

The first blow was like the sting of a thousand bees. To say that Carmella screamed behind her gag would be an understatement. Sergi paused and let the pain sink in all the way. When Carmella was on the verge of recovering her senses, he let the second blow fly. Again, she felt the piercing pain. It radiated all through her tender breasts. Her stomach was heaving with the pain. It was like being taken to another world, a kind of hell, where fire and brimstone burned to one's very core.

The other men were standing around, watching the brutal spectacle. One man had the blond girl on the ottoman, ass up, as he ploughed her pussy fiercely from behind. His grunts of passion were an unlikely background for the cracking of the cane against Carmella's mounds of pain and her muffled cries of agony.

Sergi took his time, working up and down the breasts. He would wait each time as Carmella absorbed the fierce stinging and then strike again, driving Carmella to a new height of searing pain.

Finally, Sergi was finished. Carmella hung in her chains too overwhelmed to cry. She had loved two men in her life and they had both abandoned her: Jeb and Aboud. Who would save her from this beast of a man? She would prefer to die and get it over with.

The cruel man unleashed Carmella's hands and let her fall to the floor. "Get up, slut, I've got a hard on to take care of." He nudged her side with his shoe. Carmella knew that she couldn't walk; the pain that reverberated through her body had made jelly of her muscles. But she could crawl, and so she crawled over to the ottoman where the blond girl was being fucked a moment or two before and she lifted herself up onto it, spreading her legs. She was face down, leaning on her arms to avoid contact between her sore and swollen breasts and the rough cloth of the ottoman.

Sergi stepped between Carmella's legs and pulled out his cock. It was red and hard. He slapped Carmella's ass viciously. "Stand up you worthless slut!" he ordered. "Stand up and spread your legs! Keep you hands on the stool!"

Struggling, Carmella did what she was told. Oddly, after all of the pain and torment, she was wet between the legs. Beyond all of her understanding, she craved this man's cock. When he pressed it to her pussy's lips, she moaned with rising pleasure. As he entered her, she groaned in satisfaction. Sergi pumped at Carmella's crevasse rapidly. She pushed back yearning for it to sink in all the way to her cervix. She began to cry out in frantic pleasure from behind the gag. Sergi grunted and groaned, the twenty minutes of abuse of Carmella having stoked him to a state of high excitement. He came with a loud cry, releasing a torrent of hot cum into Carmella's pussy and unleashing in her a throbbing, shattering orgasm.

Sergi's cock was still hard and he could feel the pulses of Carmella's tunnel as her orgasm subsided. He slipped his cock from her pussy and pressed it onto her ass.

Unlike the last time that he had fucked her there, this time, not only was he lubricated by their mingled discharges in her pussy, but she was ready for him, willing him to plunder her there. His thick rod spread the ring of flesh wide and pushed into her hot bowels. Carmella had never felt so aroused by the presence of a cock up her ass. It seemed that the skin around the taut ring was energized by the rubbing of the man's hot tool. She felt her passion rising again as she squeezed her buttocks and forced her anus's muscles tight around his cock. It was not long before they were both again approaching climax. Sergi reached around and grabbed Carmella's tortured tits. The intense pain served as a spark to Carmella's orgasm. She screamed as the mixture of exquisite pain and pleasure overwhelmed her. Sergi called out in his native language and shot another load of hot sperm into Carmella's body.

They were both spent. Sergi leaned on Carmella's back; she eased herself down to the ottoman, carefully avoiding crushing her breasts below her chest. After they caught their breath for a few moments, Sergi withdrew from Carmella's body and stood up. Her legs were still wide and he examined the golden disk that hung between her legs.

"Carmella, eh?" he asked no one. "Well, Carmella, you're a good fuck, I'll say that for you." He slapped her ass. "I am definitely going to see you tomorrow."

Sergi pulled his meaty weapon back into his pants and zipped up. The men in the room were silent as they tried to absorb the stark contrast between Carmella's torture and her obvious, violent outburst of pleasure. Carmella, herself, was overwhelmed. She could not explain to herself what had just happened. This man's cruel dominance of her had unlocked some door to her psyche. She had never felt more alive. She felt that she had been drawn towards some fiery center of life. She was not afraid of tomorrow, she anticipated it, wanted it. If she could not live in a world of warmth, she would live in a world of fire.

After the large man left, Carmella fucked the other men insatiably. None of them had the courage to touch her bright red tits, but they were eager to partake of the fury that Sergi had sparked in her.

Even the small, Asian attendant was set aback by the damage to Carmella's breasts. When she was returned to the dungeon, the matron at the gate made a horrified exclamation when she saw Carmella's abused mounds. She could hear the gasps of breath of the other slave girls as she was led, still blindfolded, back to the dormitory. But Carmella was proud of what she had endured. She jutted her breasts out as if they were badges of her strength and courage.

CHAPTER SEVEN

It had been seven weeks since Carmella had emerged at last from the dungeons below the House of Adeem. During those weeks she had spent about half of her waking time serving clients in the many common rooms and the other half locked below. She had not seen Aboud in all of that time. The days all merged with one another. During her time in the cellars of the whorehouse, she looked for him constantly. Her training continued and she was beaten severely twice when a guest had found her services wanting.

Sergi had kept his promise, and for three more days she absorbed his brutal assaults. Each time, when he had satisfied his wrathful lust, they fucked like tigers, their passions stoked to fiery heights. But after that, he disappeared. "Returned to the world," thought Carmella. It mattered not to her because he had shown her the way. She was not meant to endure. No, she was meant to blaze as bright and as hot as a meteor until she crashed into whatever dismal future was held in store for her.

Seventeen years. Of course she was not meant to survive it, at least not in any real sense. She had been condemned to slavery of the meanest sort by some cruel fate. Well, she would make the most of it.

Word of Carmella's passionate embrace of her slavery soon spread. Her hours in the lounge were spent sucking and fucking without respite. She would have to be virtually carried back to the dungeon, limp with exhaustion.

One day, Carmella, dressed for her duty in the lounge, was led, not there, but to another room, one in the upper floors of the palace. As she ascended the marble staircase, blindfolded, she knew that she was going somewhere new and she wondered what new cruelty awaited her there. She was surprised, when her blindfold was removed, to find herself in a large sitting room, all bedecked in white. Soft lace curtains lined the windows. The furniture was covered by bright white cushions. The rug was deep piled. At first, the room was too bright for Carmella to see anything. But then as her eyes began to become accustomed, she saw a woman sitting in a chair in front of a window. The sun shone behind her obscuring all but her outline. But then she heard a voice, a sweet, warm voice. Jennine!

"Come here, slave," Jennine called to her sweetly. Carmella walked over to her, as if in a daze. She had almost forgotten the warmth and kindness that this woman had shown her. She was the one who had bestowed the mark of the House of Adeem on her. She had comforted her and promised that they would meet again. And now they had.

Carmella fell to her knees before Jennine. Now she could see the delicate features of her face. Jennine reached out and stroked Carmella's cheek. "Carmella, you have done well," she said. "Today marks your full acceptance as a harlot in the House of Adeem. Tonight you will sleep here with me. And tomorrow we will prepare you for your new role."

She would sleep with Jennine! The coldness with which she had surrounded her heart melted. Jennine leaned over and kissed her on the lips. Carmella opened her mouth and accepted her tongue. Her hands were still bound behind her or she would have thrown herself on Jennine's knees.

"Come," Jennine said, "let me take you into the bedroom."

Carmella allowed herself to be brought to her feet. Jennine placed her finger through the ring of Carmella's collar and gently tugged, pulling her towards a large, finely sculpted door. It opened into an opulent bedroom, again all in white, with a large white bed in the middle. It was cosseted by white chiffon draperies and large fluffy pillows. Most surprisingly, there were two beautiful, languid women on the bed, dressed in long linen stoles. They were smiling at Carmella.

Carmella felt ugly amongst all this beauty; her rough, hard leather bracelets and collar, the almost comical skirt around her hips. These women wore collars and bracelets too, but theirs was made of the finest, smoothest leather, deep brown, with fine gold rings attached. They seemed bright and alive. Carmella felt her wrists being unleashed. Jennine pulled down the bright red skirt that she had been assigned that day. From behind her, Jennine stroked her breasts, proffering them to the two women on the bed.

"This is Carmella, your new sister. Isn't she lovely?" Jennine asked the two women. They affirmed Jennine's assessment with voices mellow and sensuous.

"Carmella, this is Julie and Angelina. They are here to help me welcome you to your new life," Jennine said. "Please, hop onto the bed and let them kiss you."

The young woman was beside herself with amazement. A new shock had been added to the many that she had experienced since that night at the casino. Each layer of experience had stunned her, this one not least of all. Her eyes began to tear. Could it be true? Was someone playing a mean joke on her? But as she climbed on the bed, the one called Angelina grabbed her hands and pulled her towards her. She was lean and narrow featured. She had long graceful fingers and a delicate mouth. The other, Julie, was a fiery red head, with a sparkle of freckles across her face and bright, blue eyes. Both of the women had almost shoulder length hair.

Angelina embraced Carmella, kissing her neck and pressing her bosom to her own. Julie joined them in their embrace. Carmella began to cry.

"There, there, now," Julie said, "no need to cry. This is a happy time."

Carmella was wordless. For the first time in she did not know how long, she felt she was free to speak and yet no words could come out.

Jennine spoke. "Julie and Angelina are going to give you a bath and then you will all have a delightful dinner together. Afterwards, Carmella, you will sleep with me."

Julie and Angelina, laughing, drew Carmella off of the bed and towards the bathroom. The inside of the bathroom was also white and in it lay a large, sunken tub. Angelina started the water while Julie shucked off her stole. She had firm, small breasts, with bright pink areolas. Her hips were narrow, her legs long. She guided Carmella to the toilet where she let her pee. Angelina had by now also shed her garment. Her breasts, larger than Julie's, were heavy pale mounds. The nipples were short, but broad. She was standing in the middle of the tub, the water rising rapidly. She called for Carmella to come over.

Gingerly, Carmella stepped into the soothing, hot water. Angelina grabbed a hose from the side of the tub and began to let its gentle spray flow over Carmella's body. Both of the women bore the tattoo that was the mark of the House as well as the dangling medallion in their loins. Carmella touched her own stomach as if to assure herself that hers was still there. All the women were clean shaven below and Carmella looked with desire at the slits that lay between their legs. Julie had taken out a sponge and was soaping Carmella's body. She had pressed her body up to

Carmella's back and was rubbing the sponge over her stomach and her breasts. Angelina got down on her knees before Carmella and parted her thighs. She placed her lips on Carmella's clit and sucked it gently.

Carmella sighed as the warm lips enflamed her. Julie had abandoned the sponge and was kissing the back of Carmella's neck and caressing her breasts. Carmella felt herself weaken and Julie braced her with one arm around her waist. Angelina's tongue was dipping deeply into her pussy driving her into an almost catatonic state. Never had she felt so utterly at peace since she had been literally kidnapped and despoiled by the two cops at her hotel the night that all of this had started. There were no matrons around to wield a cane. No trainers to laugh and mock her passion. She was not performing on some stage for the benefit of lecherous eyes. She was alone with two beautiful and sensuous women, being caressed and loved.

She came now, not with wild abandon, not with the throbbing, pulsing, overwhelming passion that she had become known for. This time it was gentle, soothing. Her pussy pulsed like the slow beating of a heart. A soft glow encompassed her body. She gently caressed the head that was delicately and slowly licking her purse. When she was done with her orgasm, Julie let her fall slowly into the hot, bubbly water. Angelina had thrown some bath soap into the tub and it was creating a sea of foam. The tub had a sloping wall on which to recline and Julie maneuvered Carmella to it. Angelina turned the water off and the two women lay on each side of Carmella, stroking her with their hands.

Carmella had forgotten that such moments could exist. She placed her arms around the shoulders of the two women who surrounded her and pulled them in. There was no sound in the bathroom now. The silence was almost magical as Carmella drifted into a dream-like reverie. Julie tenderly pulled Carmella's mouth over to hers and kissed her deeply. Then Angelina took her turn, thrusting her tongue into Carmella's mouth, twisting and twirling it.

Carmella's passion was rising again. She felt her legs spread wide and two hands met at the apex of her thighs. Two pairs of legs locked around hers. Angelina stuck her head under the water and began to suck on Carmella's nipple. The water was warm, but her mouth was hot. She came up for air and reclaimed Carmella's mouth. Carmella could feel her passion building now. It was not warm and gentle like before. It was a driving, heated passion, pulling into it all of Carmella's senses.

As her moment of crises was reached, Carmella cried out, her voice reverberating around the bathroom. "Oh, yes, yes, yes," she called. "Oh, fuck me, yes, fuck me, yes, yes!"

The hands at her crevasse were pushing her past her own tolerance for pleasure. Her body stiffened. She tried to pull her legs together, but the legs of the two gentle women held them tight. Her arms were trapped under the bodies of the two women who were intent on her pleasure. She uttered a loud, long moan, and then she was spent.

The three women lay there for a long time. Carmella hugged them closely, timidly kissing their faces murmuring her thanks. Twice Angelina turned on the hot water to freshen the bath. Carmella began to cry again, softly. The feeling she had now had been beyond hope for her. These gentle, loving caresses had returned to her some of her humanity. Julie whispered softly in her ear, "Later, after dinner, I want you to suck my cunt until I come. Will you do that for me?"

"Oh, yes, yes," Carmella replied. She turned to Angelina. "And you too. Can I?"

"Of course you can, Carmella," she answered. "I would love that."

After more moments of languid reverie, Julie got up and pulled the plug to the tub. As the water ran out, Angelina got out the hose and washed the soap from their bodies. She washed and rinsed Carmella's two inch long hair. Then, pulling Carmella from the tub they dried her with soft, plush towels. They led her into the bedroom and back to the bed. "We'll take a nap," Julie said, "and then we'll have dinner."

Then three women fell asleep on the soft, luxurious bed all entwined. Carmella dreamed of a different life, one far away from this cruel desert fiefdom. She was drifting on a lake, Jeb was rowing the boat, smiling, talking to her. She could not hear the words, but she felt them to be pleasant, comforting. When she awoke, it took a moment to realize where she was. At first she panicked, awaiting the crack of a cane across her breasts. But when she felt the warm, sleeping bodies next to her, she was relieved. Such peace! She knew that she was in a paradise that could not last, was not real. But she would let the waters carry her to wherever she was meant to go. She closed her eyes and drifted back to sleep.

CHAPTER EIGHT

Jeb's eyes were tired from looking at the computer monitor all day. He was reading report after report on prospective investments. In investments, knowledge is the coin of the realm and Jeb was an avid seeker of knowledge. The Prince had allowed him to effectuate some of the financial changes he had suggested and had also given him a "small" fund of $2 million to "play with". Jeb was determined to produce a short term windfall to demonstrate his value to the Prince.

Kneeling on the floor behind him was the ever present slave girl. She watched Jeb attentively, her hands behind her back, kneeling erect, her legs spread. Jeb had only to stir himself slightly and the woman, or whichever woman had been detailed to him that day, would spring to her feet to please him. Jeb was beginning to think of them as interchangeable. He had not seen the delightful slaves from the boat again, but was presented with a whole new crop when the Prince had driven him to his grand estate.

The Prince's mansion lay amidst a vast oasis. Beautiful desert palms shaded bright green grass. There were many outbuildings, stables, a paddock. The mansion itself was covered with a sandstone exterior, allowing it to blend in with the desert surroundings. Jeb had a suite of rooms to himself, a vast bedroom, an office, and a sitting room. All the furnishings were plush and luxurious. He had been given a closet full of clothing and free reign of the grounds.

Jeb spun his chair around from the computer screen and stretched his arms and legs. The brown haired slave perked at his movements and jumped to her feet. "How may I serve you, Master?" she said, her head bowed low, her legs invitingly spread. He had seen this one before, Nina or Natalie or something like that. Her taut stomach displayed the mark of Adeem, a bright blue, cursive "A" surrounded by intricate flourishes. Was Carmella out there somewhere sporting a similar brand? At whose feet did she serve?

Jeb dared not ask the Prince for assistance in finding Carmella. He could not divulge his true identity or he would almost certainly end up on a spike, or tethered to posts in the desert until the sun baked him to a crispy brown. He had been able to make contact over the Internet with certain people, who knew people, who knew people. He had been able to raise just enough cash of his own to find out who needed to be bribed. But he needed more cash desperately if he was ever going to get the information he needed most: where was Carmella?

It was strange to live a life of almost perpetual sexual arousal. Everywhere he went, the dining room, the hallways, his suite, even in the lush gardens that surrounded the mansion, there were naked, beautiful, willing women. Every night he took one or more of them to his bed. Each time, he was driven to almost furious passion by their expert and enthusiastic lovemaking.

Jeb looked at the expectant slave girl. She was beautifully rounded. She had a pleasant, soft face. Her breasts shook slightly, invitingly, as she stood, awaiting a command.

"Bring me your breasts," he ordered. The girl smiled and stepped closer to him, leaning over and cupping the underside of her breasts, proffering them to him. He took a nipple in his mouth and circled the other breast with his hand. The girl was gently scented, and he breathed deeply, stirred by the delicate fragrance. Her nipples were now hard. She moaned lowly.

Jeb released the nipple from his mouth and spoke to the girl, "Take my prick in your mouth."

She knelt between his knees and undid his pants. Jeb was already hard and she plunged her mouth down its length. Her tongue circled it as she sucked on the swollen shaft. She grabbed his balls with her hand and caressed them gently. Jeb closed his eyes and sighed. He couldn't help but think of Carmella on her knees before him, obedient, passionate. Jeb had lost all patience for coyness or reticence. Many weeks of unremitting pleasure from highly desirable women, women who were delighted to obey any command, had changed Jeb. "How can I ever go back to a world where women like these did not exist?" he thought to himself.

He felt his crisis coming and started to pump his cock to meet the slave girl's passionate attentions. He could delay it no longer and his cock throbbed with exquisite pleasure. He felt his seed shoot into the exuberant mouth.

When he was done, the girl dutifully massaged his cock with her lips to extract every drop of cum. When he became tumescent, she raised her head from Jeb's lap with an appreciative grin on her face. She had pleasured him, fulfilled her duty, her only reason for existence.

The telephone rang. Timing was everything. Jeb, after restoring his cock and balls to his pants, picked up the receiver. It was Rashid, the Prince's major domo. Since the Prince had gone off to who knows where, all of Jeb's dealings had been with Rashid. Any proposal he made for fiscal action, every request for information or for access to resources went through Rashid. Sometimes he would answer, "As you propose, it shall be done." Other times he would hesitate momentarily and say, "I must consult the

Prince." And an hour or two later Jeb would have his answer.

Ever since he started to deal with the Prince's investments in earnest, Jeb had been lobbying for an assistant. He had been told that the Prince had approved his request, but still no assistant had been forthcoming. Jeb needed someone to keep track of all the information he was compiling, to type and forward letters of request, to monitor and report on certain trends, to remind him of deadlines and checkpoints he had set for himself to determine when to buy or sell.

Rashid, as usual, addressed him formally. "Mr. Turner, would you be so kind as to come to the first floor reception room. I have some candidates for your assistant for you to see."

At last. "Of course, Rashid," Jeb replied, "I'll be right down.

The mansion was so huge that it took Jeb several minutes to get there. One of the ubiquitous, tall, black and inscrutable guards stood outside the door and let him in. What Jeb saw was not what he expected. Lined up, side to side, along the far wall of the reception room, were four young white women. They were all naked. Their hands were behind their heads and they were all standing erect. Before each one of them was a small pile of women's clothes, blouses, skirts, bras and underwear. They were all still wearing their stockings and high-heeled shoes.

"Ah, Mr. Turner, thank you for your alacrity. I believe that one of these women will suit your needs very well," Rashid addressed Jeb politely.

Jeb was somewhat taken aback. These were not slave girls, since they wore neither bracelets nor collars. Their pubic hair was unshorn and their hair was, for the most part, long and unclipped. To a one, their eyes were red and wet, and darting around the room nervously.

The women were all shapely and pleasant of face. They were young, but somewhat older than the average age of the slaves that he had seen. As Jeb approached them Rashid made an explanation.

"These women are all very experienced administrative assistants. They have been brought here from New York so that you might pick one as your secretary. I assure you that they are all very competent and will serve your needs well."

One of the girl's was sniffling. She had a red stripe across her breasts and Jeb assumed that she had needed some persuasion to obey and keep silent. As he perused the women, Jeb realized that he had not given his request for assistance much thought as to where that person might be found. He knew that no male native would deign to serve under the supervision of an infidel like him. Had he really thought about it, he would have realized that it would be difficult to find a woman to assist him who would not blanch at the surroundings and atmosphere in which she would have to work. No Westerner, except those sworn to self-interested secrecy, was permitted in the security zone in which the Prince's mansion, his whorehouse and all the other whorehouses where women served as slaves, existed. Once there, no unanswered for Western woman could ever be allowed to leave.

"Let me brief you on the background and experience of these sluts," Rashid proffered to Jeb. He walked up to the first one. She had long blond hair, was tall and had long shapely legs. Her breasts were small and firm. Her pubic hair was delicate, like a wisp. Her eyes were blue and her features sharp and graceful.

"This is Emily. She spent the last two years working for the Security and Exchange Commission. She has a B.A. in business from Loyola College. She is 25 years old."

The girl stared wide-eyed as her curriculum vita was discussed. Rashid moved on to the next girl. She had dark brown hair that ended in soft, wavy curls at her shoulders. Her eyes were brown and she had wide, full lips. Her hips were broad, her legs short. She stood about 5'5" in her heels. Her breasts were large and heavy with short, wide nipples. They were stiff with fear and apprehension.

"This is Rhonda. She is 26 years old and spent the last seven years working in the research department of Morgan, Stanley. She is very capable and has strong recommend-dations."

He moved on to the third girl. She also had shoulder length hair, but black and straight. Her complexion was pale, her skin appeared soft and sensitive. She was the one who had been sniffling and she started anew as Jeb and Rashid approached her. Rashid was holding a small riding crop and he patted her gently rising breasts with it. She needed no further warning and stopped her emotional outpouring. Her face was round, her lips poutish. She was well toned.

"Amy has held several jobs over the past five years. She worked for a couple of investment houses and then worked for a major broker. She too is well recommended. She is a little older than the rest, but is in fine physical form."

Rashid then came to the last girl. She was slight of form, not quite skinny, but very thin. She was another brunette and her hair was close cropped. Her breasts were a little out of proportion to her slender frame. But what stood out most of all were the rings in her nipples.

"I am afraid that our information on this slut was somewhat deficient. If I had known in advance that she had defaced her body, she would never have made it past the first interview. But, since she has come all of this way, I thought it best to present her, if only as a contrast to the others."

The nameless girl was crying silently, tears running down her face. Her almost green eyes nervously looked away from the two men who were brazenly admiring her naked body.

"Open your mouth!" Rashid commanded the girl. Reluctantly, the girl opened her mouth. In the middle of her tongue was a small silver ball. Her face reddened as evidence of her humiliation. She started to shake.

"And her clit has been pierced," Rashid added. "Spread your legs!" he ordered her.

The petit girl widened her thighs. Her bush was neatly trimmed and Jeb could see the ring that pierced her bud.

"To her credit, this slut has very good experience. She has two years of law school and was on sabbatical, working for the U.S. attorney's office as an intern, as incongruent as that may seem. The greedy whore was enticed by the promise of a generous salary," Rashid said. "She has been tested, as have they all, and she is free of any disease, but as you can imagine, she has been well used. I have to say that if you do not select her, and I do not want to influence your decision in any way, I would find it most amusing to indulge her penchant for bodily piercing to an extreme. But of course, it is up to you. If you select her, she will be yours to use and dispose of."

Jeb realized that this was probably his best opportunity to acquire a competent assistant. Not only that, he realized that the sole reason these women had been somehow enticed to come to Calipha had been his request for help. If he turned them down, within a week or two, four new hapless beauties would be standing here, naked and trembling.

But still, he found it hard to make a decision. "What will happen to the ones that I don't pick," he asked Rashid.

"We will keep them around until you are sure the one you have selected will suit you. Afterwards, they could be used as house slaves, serving wenches. We do need to make provision for the sexual urges of the staff. Or they could be sold along to one of the lesser houses. They are really a little older than we would consider for the House of Adeem. On the other hand, the blonde," he looked back at the clearly distressed naked woman, "well, perhaps. But anyway, that is no concern of yours. Pick the one you like best. They are all competent and qualified."

Jeb strolled back and forth in front of the hapless young women. He liked the blond and imagined her long legs wrapped around him. The second girl, the brunette was nice, with succulent lips. But the forlorn visage of the third girl was the most tempting. She had an innocence of expression that contrasted sharply with her predicament. He also felt that she would be the most compliant, the most ready to fulfill his instructions without delay or complaint.

Rashid spoke to the girls, "Turn around." To Jeb he said, "You must see them from the back."

The women dutifully shuffled their feet and turned so that their backs were to Jeb and Rashid. "Bend over and touch your toes!" he commanded. "Spread you legs!"

Rashid had a harsh voice when he wanted to, belying his usual soft spoken and demure demeanor.

The prisoners all obeyed. Jeb was confronted with four wide-open, luscious posteriors.

"Sometimes you need to explore the cunt to get a good feel for the slave," he said to Jeb. "Feel between their legs and see if that will help your decision."

The blond woman uttered a quiet squeal when Jeb took hold of the flesh between her legs. She was dry and it took some manipulation of her lips and her bud to moisten her. The second one too was dry. But the third girl, Amy, her pussy was lush and soft. He could see the prominent lips flush with blood. She moaned as he stroked her. He didn't need to go any further.

"This one," Jeb said. "I'll take this one."

Rashid ordered the other girls to stand up and turn back around. There were three of the muscular guards in the room and Rashid ordered two of them to take the first two girls away. Rashid ordered the fourth one, the slight, slender girl with the pierced nipples, to go down on her hands and knees and to crawl over to the corner. He left her there, head into the corner, her tight ass presented.

Amy was still doubled over. Jeb could hear her crying. Little did she know that she was undoubtedly the luckiest of the four. Jeb had no idea what Rashid had in mind for the pierced girl, but the first two were certainly destined for one or the other of the local whorehouses and a period of abusive, dehumanizing training. Amy would be working with him and, apart from the occasional fuck, her duties would be light.

Rashid gave a nod to the remaining guard, a large black skinned fellow with a face full of ritualistic scars. He was just about the meanest thing Jeb had ever seen.

The guard went over to a closet and removed a large, thick leather collar and four bracelets. He approached Amy without further instruction and placed two of the bracelets around her ankles. Rashid then ordered her to stand and turn back around. Tears were running down her cheeks, her face showing her extreme dismay. This was certainly not what she had in mind when she answered the N.Y. Times ad offering an exciting overseas posting in an exotic locale. It was surreal: the Arabian Nights décor, the chains, the whips.

The guard affixed the bracelets to Amy's wrists and then fastened them behind her back. Her eyes bulged when she saw the large, thick leather collar. The guard snapped it around her neck. More tears flowed. Amy summoned the courage to speak.

"What are you doing with me? Please let me go!" she asked plaintively. Her voice was slightly more than a whisper, high pitched, desperate. "I want to go home," she cried. "I haven't done anything wrong. Please, please, don't do this to me!"

Rashid quickly lashed her breasts with the riding crop. The room resounded with the loud "crack!" Amy bent over doubled and wailed. "Ohhhhhhhhhhhhh!"

The guard pulled her back up straight by her hair. She stood on her tiptoes, blubbering.

"Silence!" commanded Rashid. He let her have another stroke. She cried out in pain, but held back her sobs.

Rashid turned to Jeb. "Faisal will take charge of her for forty eight hours. She will be presented to you for her work the day after tomorrow. Don't worry, she will be obedient and will follow all of your instructions earnestly. Do you want to fuck her before Faisal takes her below?"

Jeb was sorely tempted. He recalled lustfully the soft, hot pussy he had discovered between her legs. For some reason, though, he didn't want to be the first to rape this newly enslaved girl. For some reason, he could make a distinction between imposing his lust on a female who had been broken to her enslavement and fucking a girl against her will who still retained the sensibilities of a free woman.

"No," Jeb answered. "Let Faisal take her. I'll fuck her when she is presented to me for work."

Rashid made a waving gesture at Faisal. He snapped a leash on Amy's collar and led her away.

CHAPTER NINE

Carmella lay on a large, flowered ottoman, her legs splayed, perspiration glistening on her body. Her breathing was heavy, her naked breasts trembling at the rise and fall of her chest. Her eyelids were fluttering. The long, diaphanous skirt that she wore was spread around her. The lips of her sex were engorged, its center flush and dilated, leaking fluids.

The tall, lean man, with dark hair and a sharp featured face who had been passionately using her had risen and was seeking out his clothing. "You're a good fuck, Carmella," he said. "I'll be back here next month and I'll look you up." Carmella floated back to consciousness. She had been fucking with this man for three hours. She didn't know his name. He had picked her out from the slave catalogue that morning and she had been delivered to his room right after lunch, bedecked in her flowing skirt, naked from the waist up. Her hair had grown longer now and, although still short, had been teased into tiny ringlets. Her eyes had been highlighted with dark liner, her pale cheeks rouged lightly. Her eyelids were colored with a light blue shadow. A light spray of a musky perfume had been applied to her body.

As was the custom, she had awaited the arrival of her unknown admirer kneeling, with her wrists locked behind her back, her collar affixed with a chain to the foot of the bed.

When the gentleman had entered, Carmella had presented herself to him. She arched her back so that her breasts stood out to their advantage. Her knees were spread wide, so that the outline of her hairless sex could be discerned beneath her sheer silk skirt. Her eyes were downcast, as befitted a slave.

The man stepped close to Carmella. She could only see the light brown leather shoes that he wore and bottom of his cream colored slacks. He was apparently taking a moment to appreciate her body.

This was the moment that Carmella dreaded the most of these encounters. Arrayed before her on the floor was a selection of three instruments of torture: a long, single lashed whip, one with seven thick, knotted cords and a long, thin reed. She had stared at them for the last 45 minutes while she awaited the arrival of her client. She knew their uses well. It was the guest's privilege to decide if she was to be beaten.

He had not beaten her. Apparently, this was his first experience at the House of Adeem. He was hesitant, almost apologetic at first, as he caressed her breasts. When he spoke, Carmella realized that he was a fellow American, uttering his English with that flat, almost nasal accent. He was probably from the Midwest. Certainly nothing he had experienced in the Corn Belt had prepared him for this.

Americans were few and far between among the House's guests. Americans were generally disdained in this Muslim nation.

Since the night she had spent in Jennine's bed, Carmella had served at a much higher level of elegance and refinement. The night she slept with Jennine, Jennine had removed her thick leather confinements. For one night she had reexperienced the delight of being free from her bonds. Three times during the night their bodies had joined. Jennine's use of her was firm, but tender. Carmella followed her lead as she was urged to proffer her breasts, spread her thighs. She delighted herself at Jennine's cunt, absorbing the deep musty smell of Jennine's arousal. Carmella, pleasurably exhausted, nestled in Jennine's arms and slept.

In the morning, Jennine had outfitted her with the sleek, polished leather bindings that Julie and Angelina wore. Carmella tearfully, but passively, accepted their imposition on her body. For one night she had been free, or so it had seemed. She had caressed Jennine willingly, as a lover would and had received Jennie's caresses in the same way. But the fantasy was now dispelled. Jennine took note of her dismay.

"Carmella, nothing that has happened here has changed the fact that you are a slave. You must remember that always, or you will be returned to the cellars and suffer another period of extended torment." She was stroking Carmella's hair as she spoke.

"I am your mistress and my duty is to see to it that you serve our Master's guests with all of the eagerness and skill that you have been taught."

Carmella gazed tearfully at her mistress. Of course, nothing had changed. She was a slave, an 'object of pleasure', as she had been told repeatedly. For just a moment, however, lost in the reveries of the past few hours, she had forgotten that.

Jennine joined Carmella's wrists before her. "I am going to whip you now, Carmella, so that you know that I rule you as much as any other of the trainers or matrons or guards of this House. You are a beautiful, lustful creature and I appreciate that as much as anyone here. But nonetheless, you are to obey me, and suffer my whims and commands as much as any other master or guest."

Carmella nodded her affirmation of the harsh words she had heard, words that were spoken in the soft and caressing tones of a sensuous, desirable woman, but one who was as committed to the enforcement of her baseness and degradation as anyone.

Jennine led Carmella to a chain that hung from the ceiling. She locked Carmella's wrists to the chain and pulled it up, leaving Carmella dangling, her toes barely touching the floor.

Jennine produced a long leather thong. She pressed her naked body up next to Carmella's. "Sweet one," she whispered in Carmella's ear, "I'm going to give you ten lashes with this whip. I want to hear you scream as loud as you want. When I am done, you will kiss me and thank me."

Carmella uttered a tremulous affirmation of her instructtions. And she did scream loudly as Jennine tormented her body with the lash. She cried out her despair at her terrible misfortunes. She cried out her outrage at the abuse she was suffering. She cried out her love for Jennine, her obedience to her, her acceptance of her fate.

When the whipping was done, Jennine placed her lips on Carmella's and thrust her tongue deeply into her mouth. Carmella returned the kiss, grateful to be possessed by this strict, yet tender woman. She thanked her for her beating with all of her heart.

The next few days, Carmella was acclimated to her new role. She was now among the elite of the slaves of the House of Adeem. She would be permitted clothing, but only that which was of a nature to present her beauteous assets to their best and most seductive advantage. She was photographed in the most suggestive and lewd poses, for the perusal and titillation of the House's preferred guests.

She was instructed on her duties. She would share a bed with another slave, but they would have their own room. Sex between them was encouraged. In fact, the rule of the

House as it pertained to guests also pertained in the upstairs dormitory area. No slave was permitted to deny a demand for sexual services by any other slave. This was sometimes the source of conflict as, naturally, some slaves were considered more desirable than others, depending on your point of view. But all conflicts were resolved amicably, or they were resolved by Jennine using the end of a whip.

The girls who lived in these upper floors were graceful, beautiful creatures. Their smiles could melt hearts, create an aching, longing feeling, the springboard of desire. But all in all, they were still whores. Owned flesh. They could be rented by the hour or by the day. They often served as dinner partners at parties. If not assigned to a guest, they would congregate in the finely appointed bar and lounge. A guest could cruise the bar, chat up one of the refinely coiffured ladies and take her upstairs to the guest rooms. They could still be beaten or abused, as the guest saw fit, but largely they were wanted for their skillful and passionate sexual services. The bill would be presented deferentially by one of the staff as the guest left.

Carmella was paired off, initially, with a red headed girl named Kathy. The bed sharing arrangements were shifted every few weeks. Although the girls were strictly forbidden to speak about their pasts, Carmella deduced that she was Irish from her accent and by the length of her hair that she had been a slave for a little longer than Carmella had. They did not often use the bed at the same time since the vagaries of the demands of the guests prevented them from having the same schedule. But when they did, they made passionate love to each other. At night they were chained by their collars to the headboard and their hands were affixed to their collars. Thus, being denied the use of their hands, they would kiss passionately, pressing their bodies together and scissoring their legs so that they could rub their pussies against each other's. The elite whores were permitted one day off per week and it was on those days that they could find a partner for prolonged lovemaking. Being new, Carmella was in high demand. Thus she got to know the other inmates of this exotic gnyceum quickly.

Carmella developed a crush on a little blond haired girl, a Dane, with ethereal features and small delicate breasts. Whenever she could, she would seek her out and spend hours caressing her, licking her quim and being licked in return.

But most of the time it was the demands of the guests that were satisfied. Since the cost of utilizing the "upstairs girls", as they were called, was high, the demand for services, although steady, was less than Carmella had experienced as a "lounge girl". She would still service, on a normal day, two or three different men, but the service was more ritualistic, more formal. Carmella could spend an hour sucking a cock, running her lips all over a man's body. She had learned how to prolong a man's pleasure and, after he had spilled his seed in her mouth, her pussy or her ass, as he preferred, she knew how to excite him, after a brief respite, to climb the mountain once again.

Most of the clients were either wealthy Arabs or Europeans. Once in a while, she would be chosen for use by an American. To hear the flat, nasal use of English was disconcerting. Carmella kept her thoughts as far away as she could from her former life. To hear an American accent was to bring her forcibly back to her life as a free woman.

The first time that she had been confronted with the assignment of servicing an American had been, perhaps, the most disconcerting of all. It was rare that women would appear as guests, but it was not unknown. On this day, Carmella had been reserved for an afternoon assignation. She, of course, had no idea who she would fuck. She just knew that her most enthusiastic and professional services would be required.

She had been affixed to the foot of the bed when the couple entered. They entered talking and Carmella knew right away that they were Americans. She could only see their feet and the bottom portion of their clothes when they entered, but she could hear their flat, almost tepid English. Their voices were light and airy like two vacationers on a stroll. The woman spoke first.

"Bill, she's beautiful. You were right, she's perfect."

Bill had stopped a foot or so away from Carmella. "I told you. Look at those tits, they're gorgeous."

Carmella blushed slightly at the complement. She could never get used to the frank appraisal of her body and never really got used to presenting her naked breasts to strangers.

"Oh, and look at these whips!" The woman's voice was high pitched and nasal. She was wearing smart leather sandals. As she leaned over to pick up a whip, Carmella caught a whiff of a flowery perfume. She stole a look at the woman. She was wearing a clinging shift of soft cotton that reached down to just below her knees. It was a soft beige, appropriate for this desert clime. She had a broad, almost plain face, but her finely applied makeup highlighted her high cheekbones and the sharp outlines of her eyes.

The woman stood up and Carmella could hear the "whoosh" of a whip as it was swung through the air.

"Oh, Bill, this is incredible! We have to whip her! I want to do it. Can I?"

"Anything you want Liz," Bill replied. "Anything you want."

"Let's stand her up. I want to see all of her."

"Then tell her. She'll do what you say. Don't be embarrassed, she's used to this."

"Okay. What was her name again?"

"Carmella."

"Yeah, Carmella. Okay. Carmella, I order you to stand up."

"Honey, she's locked to the bed. You have to release her chain first," Bill told his companion.

"You do it," she replied. "Unlock her."

Carmella was wearing a flowing, sheer, silk skirt, covered with a flowery design, ankle length. When she stood up, the skirt danced about her legs. Carmella kept her eyes focused towards the floor.

"Oh, she's beautiful, Bill. And look at the design on her stomach. She's really a slave?"

"Oh, very much so," Bill replied. "In every sense of the word."

"This is so exquisite!" Liz exclaimed. "I need a drink."

Carmella knew that she needed to assume control of events. She knew that she needed to project her reality as a person to her 'clients' so that this would be more than an impersonal exchange of bodily fluids. Guests of the House of Adeem were entitled to more than that.

And so she spoke. "If it pleases the madam and the gentleman, I will pour them some cold, white wine," she said.

Liz was taken aback. The fact that this creature spoke broke some preconceived notion of how a slave should behave. But Carmella knew her business. She knew that the more personal she could make the experience, the more exciting it would be and the less likely she would be unmercifully abused.

Bill apparently had been to the House before. "Pour us two wines, slave. And then remove your skirt."

"As the gentleman wishes," Carmella replied.

She went over to the sideboard, careful to grace each step with a sensuous motion. She poured two glasses of golden white wine and proffered them to Liz and Bill.

Taking the glass from Carmella, Liz watched, entranced, as Carmella smoothly shucked the skirt from her body. She stood as she had been trained, legs apart, back arched. Her breasts jutted from her chest, proffered to the use of the guests.

Bill was the first to react. He took a swig of his wine and, placing the glass on a small table near the bed, stepped behind Carmella. He snaked his hands around her waist, pressing up against her rear, and began to fondle her breasts. He pushed them up and squeezed the nipples. His cock was hard, and rubbed up against her ass.

Liz watched in silence. She sipped at her wine as Bill manipulated the nipples on Carmella's breasts to hardness. He kissed her neck and ran his hand down her stomach, down to her moistening sex.

"Well, Liz," he said, looking up at his companion, "you said you wanted to whip her."

"Oh, yes," Liz replied in a sultry voice. "I want to whip her right now."

"First you have to take off your clothes. I want to see you naked while you're whipping her."

"You too, Bill. It's only fair."

Carmella stood silently as the two Americans disrobed. She watched Liz intently, jealous of the woman's freedom. Liz wriggled out of her shift revealing small white panties and a push up bra. She espied Carmella's interest and spoke to her harshly. "Don't look at me you whore! Turn your back!"

Carmella was startled at the woman's hostility. She immediately deflected her eyes and turned around. Bill, who was standing in his underwear and socks, laughed.

"Don't worry honey. She won't tell anyone," Bill said, amused at Liz's modesty.

"She was staring at me," Liz replied. "She doesn't have the right to stare at me!"

"Of course she doesn't," said Bill. "You have to punish her for that."

Carmella felt a knot in her stomach. This woman was going to really beat her. She would never get used to being beaten, especially by those motivated by malice. She recalled Sergi and his four day spree of torture. What twisted, perverted soul had driven him, she did not know. But she had not sensed such meanness since.

Bill and Liz were now fully disrobed. Liz leaned up against Bill and kissed him passionately. "Oh, Bill, this is so exciting! Chain her up, I can't wait!"

Bill grabbed Carmella's hands and joined them together. He pulled her over to the chain that descended from the ceiling of the room and affixed them there. He then pulled the other end of the chain until Carmella's hands were up in the air and she was standing on her toes. He locked the chain in place.

Liz had picked up the tasseled whip and was measuring its weight in her hand. Carmella, although keeping her eyes lowered, stole a glance and saw an almost dumpy, thick thighed woman. Her breasts, while ample, sagged slightly. There was a small ring of fat around her hips. Unlike Carmella, this was a woman who looked best clothed.

The woman approached Carmella and looked her in the eyes. Carmella could see the woman's building passion. Liz saw Carmella's fear and apprehension. "Oh, Bill," she exclaimed, "I can't believe this is real. Where do they get these girls anyway?"

"You're better off not knowing, Liz. Just be thankful that you're not one of them."

"Can I touch her? I want to feel her body first."

"It's all in the price of admission, honey. Let yourself go."

Liz dropped the whip momentarily and placed her hands on Carmella's breasts. Her touch was delicate at first, hesitant. Carmella's nipples rose. Liz pressed harder on her breasts, caressing them firmly now.

"It's just like I'm touching myself. It's weird," Liz said.

Bill had poured himself another glass of wine and was watching intently. Corruption starts with small steps and he was watching the first steps of this woman down that road. Liz bent over and took one of Carmella's nipples in her mouth. She sucked at it, running her tongue across the tip. She switched to the other breast and Carmella let out a soft moan as the heat of arousal began in her. Liz looked up at Carmella and smiled. "I know just how you feel, honey," she said to Carmella.

She ran her hands down Carmella's sides to her hips. "Look at this tattoo!" she remarked to Bill. "Oh, it's beautiful. What does it mean?"

Bill was massaging his fully erect cock. His eyes were focused on the picture of his naked companion exploring Carmella's flesh. "It's an "A", for the House of Adeem, the name of this place," he said. "She belongs to the House of Adeem."

"No, silly, the writing underneath. It's in Arabic or something."

"I don't really know. I've never asked. 'I am the property of the House of Adeem', I suppose. 'Return postage guaranteed.'"

Liz laughed. "Very funny. I don't think she would fit in a post box."

"You're right. So maybe it says something else. But come on, I want to fuck this bitch and I'm getting pretty randy here."

"Okay, okay, but I haven't finished looking at her yet."

Liz crouched on her haunches and took a long look at Carmella's hairless mound. "I've never looked at a cunt from this angle before," she said. "Without the hair, it's beautiful. And she's pierced. There's a tag."

She fingered the tag and read Carmella's name off of it. "Carmella. What's that, in case she forgets?" Liz asked sarcastically.

"No, it's in case she's gagged and you want to know her name."

"Gagged?"

"Yeah, like if you don't want to hear her yell and scream when she's beaten."

"It's just odd. I just didn't think about slaves having a name. It makes it more personal."

"Well, whipping her is going to be very personal."

Liz replied in a low, husky voice, "Yeah, very personal. Anyway, I don't want her gagged. I want to hear her yell."

She spread Carmella's thighs to get a better look at her naked pussy. She leaned over and ran her tongue along the outer lips. Carmella squirmed at the tantalizing feeling of the other woman's tongue. Liz placed her hand on Carmella's sex and parted the lips. "She's wet!" Liz exclaimed. "She's fucking wet!"

Liz pressed her fingers deep inside Carmella's moist pussy. "She is a whore. A regular lust machine," Liz giggled.

Liz stood up and circled behind Carmella. She ran her hands across Carmella's ass. She pressed her body against Carmella's and circled her arms around Carmella's front, grabbing her tits, mauling them. "I'm going to whip you honey," she whispered in Carmella's ear. "Right here on your tits. And everywhere else too. Does that make you hot?"

Carmella, disconcerted by the thought that this presumably civilized American couple could discuss whipping her with such callousness, replied in as neutral a voice as she could muster, "If it pleases the madam."

"Oh, yes, very much," Liz hissed.

Finally, she stood away from Carmella and retrieved the whip she had dropped. She swung it twice in the air, listening to its "whoosh". "I'll be that this hurts like hell," she said.

"I'd wager it does," replied Bill. "So do it already. Lost your nerve?"

"Oh, no, I haven't lost my nerve," Liz said, turning towards Carmella. "Whoosh", the whip sliced through the air, its leather tassels striking Carmella across her breasts. Carmella stiffened. Another blow descended. "Crack!" Now, Carmella winced. A third blow across her breasts and she uttered a low moan.

Cruelty resides in every soul and Liz was no exception. Take away the limits of civilized society and you will find out who you really are. Liz rained blow after blow on Carmella's tits, not pausing for respite. If she was waiting for Carmella's cries and wails, she succeeded because Carmella did cry and wail. She hated being whipped, more than the humiliation, the degradation, the casual use and abuse of her body. She hated the pain that made an enemy of her own flesh. And at the hands of this spoiled and careless bitch! If she hadn't been chained she would have leapt at her, striking her down. But she was chained, helpless. She could only suffer, and she would, too, for so long as this witch meant her to.

Liz finished with the breasts and descended to Carmella's thighs. She was really into it now, sweat glistening on her body, her own tits swinging wildly as she raised and lowered her arm with all of her might. Bill was taking it in. He knew that she would never be the same. She was hooked. She would relive this moment a hundred times. And she would want it again and again.

Carmella was crying now, holding back with all her strength the begging and pleading to be spared. Her feet leapt with each blow to her thighs. She tried to press them together to protect her tender sex.

"Bill, pull her legs apart. I want to whip her cunt!" Liz's face was red with passion. She had lost control of her lust. She wanted this whore to suffer.

Bill spread Carmella's legs and tied them off to two rings that lay attached to the floor. Carmella's legs were splayed, ready for the whip.

It was a difficult angle, but Liz managed to land several blows directly on Carmella's tender pussy. Carmella's resolve not to plead and beg dissipated. "Ohhhhhhhhhh!, please, stop, please!" she cried out. "Oh, god, please! Please!" Carmella writhed and danced in her chains.

This was what Liz had been looking for. With fire in her eyes, she directed blow after blow to Carmella's loins. Finally, as Liz raised the whip back to strike again, Bill took hold of her arm. She looked at him, dazed. Carmella was sobbing, her breasts and pussy afire. "Let's fuck her now," Bill said softly to Liz.

"Okay," Liz whispered back, momentarily exhausted.

Bill tossed the whip aside and unloosened Carmella's bonds. It took a moment for her to steady herself. She too was drenched with sweat.

She felt herself dragged over to the bed. Bill pushed her onto it and joined her there. Liz followed. Carmella felt

Bill's sex plunge deep into her own. She was wet and ready. On her back, her legs spread wide, Carmella let her passion carry her away.

"No, turn her over," Liz cried. "I want her to suck my cunt!"

Bill obliged, withdrawing his hot prick and flipping Carmella to her stomach. He raised her hips and again plunged his long, hard dick into her moist sheath.

Liz had maneuvered herself below Carmella's head and pulled her down to her crotch. "Suck my cunt you fucking whore!" she ordered.

Carmella obediently pressed her mouth against Liz's hot pussy. Liz had her legs spread wide and put her hands on Carmella's head. "Suck my clit!" she yelled. "Eat my pussy! Eat it! Eat it!"

Her own passions rising to the point of crisis, Carmella energetically administered her mouth and tongue to Liz's sex. Her hips were rocking back and forth to meet Bill's thrusts. She wanted his come inside her. She wanted to feel him pulse and jerk in her pussy and splash his hot semen inside. All three of them came at once, each moaning or yelling their passions aloud. Liz yelped with pleasure as she squeezed Carmella's head with her thighs. Bill groaned as he spent his load deep into Carmella's canal. And Carmella moaned her passions deep inside Liz's gushing pussy.

The three lay in a heap for several seconds. Liz stirred first. "Oh," she said, "that was too much!" Carmella's head was still in her lap. "And the whore came too!"

Bill was still lazily stroking his rapidly decompressing cock in Carmella's slit. "Oh, yeah, she feels good."

Liz slapped Carmella's face lightly. "Who told you to stop, slave?" Her accent on the last word was contemptuous. Carmella winced inwardly at the woman's cruel manner, but dutifully started lapping again. It was not long before Liz was again moaning and squirming as a result of Carmella's expert tonguing of her crevasse. Though humiliated and ashamed, she knew her duty and what would happen to her if these boorish Americans complained.

Bill watched silently as Liz reached her second climax. She bucked her hips into Carmella's mouth, moaning and groaning. Finally she pushed Carmella's head aside. "Oh, that's enough. My cunt can't take it."

Carmella knelt back on her heels awaiting further instructions. Bill ordered her to serve them some more wine. She rose from the bed to comply.

"I want to watch her suck your cock," she said to Bill.

"Give me a few moments, Liz."

Carmella handed the two guests their wine and stood away from the bed. Liz looked up at her. "I told you not to look at me. Go stand in the corner!"

Carmella nodded her head dutifully and stepped over to the corner of the room and turned her back on the couple, placing her hands dutifully behind her back.

"Why are you so harsh with her?" Bill asked.

"Because she's a stupid cunt!"

"Why do you say that?"

"Any woman who'd let herself be made into a fucking sex slave is a stupid cunt, that's why!"

"I don't think she had much choice in it Liz," Bill commented.

"There's always a choice, Bill."

There's always a choice thought Carmella. Yes, that's true. She chose life as a slave rather than pain and probably death. She was a stupid cunt. She was the lowest of the low. A tear rolled down her cheek. What did this woman know? How would she react to the lash and the abuse she had suffered? Carmella stared at the wall, hating Liz, hating herself.

"Lighten up, Liz," Bill said. He called to Carmella. "Come here Carmella."

Carmella, mortified by the tear on her cheek obeyed.

Bill wiped it away with his hand. "Carmella is a very good whore. That's what she is. She can't help it. Can you Carmella?"

"No, sir," she murmured.

"Come and suck my dick."

Bill sat at the head of the bed propped up by pillows as Carmella maneuvered herself between his knees. Liz, wineglass in hand, sat next to Bill, watching intently.

Carmella tenderly stroked the head of Bill's cock with her tongue and then took the sensitive knob into her mouth. Bill moaned with pleasure. Liz leaned over and kissed him, rubbing his chest. Carmella worked slowly and expertly at pleasuring Bill's now rock hard meat. She was determined to make Bill moan louder and come harder than Liz could ever do. She was a good whore. One of the best.

Liz's hand was in her pussy as she watched as Carmella's mouth work up and down Bill's cock. She watched with amazement as Carmella took it all down her throat. Bill was moaning loudly, calling, "Yes! Yes! Yes! Oh, god!"

His hand was on Carmella's head and his other hand was wrapped around Liz's waist. Liz kissed him again, their mouths merging as Carmella began to take Bill over the top. As she felt his cock throb, she pushed it all the way down her throat. Bill's hips bucked and shuddered as he came.

"Well," Liz said approvingly afterwards, "She really is a good whore. I hope you don't expect that from me."

Bill was still enraptured from the blowjob. "Eh?" he said.

"Never mind," Liz said. Carmella had released Bill's cock and was kneeling between his legs. Liz stroked her hair. "I'm sorry honey if I hurt your feelings."

Carmella was afraid to look at her. "Yes, madam."

"Come here and let me kiss you." Carmella leaned over Bill's leg and proffered her lips to Liz. Liz placed a tender kiss on them and, taking hold of her arm, pulled her closer. She pried Carmella's lips apart with her tongue and entered her mouth. Carmella's body responded and she kissed her back. Soon the women's bodies were intertwined. Their breasts rubbed against each others', their hips ground together. She turned Carmella over on her back and ran her hand down her stomach to her hot, wet canal. Carmella shivered as Liz played with her clit, kissing her breasts. Bill reached in a hand and pulled Carmella's thighs apart.

Liz came up for air. "Can you get it up again, Bill?"

"I got hard just watching you two," he replied.

"I want you to fuck her in the ass."

"And what will you be doing?"

"I'm going to stroke her cunt. I want to watch it when she comes."

"Turn her over," Bill instructed.

"No, do it this way. Raise her legs."

Bill raised Carmella's legs and Liz slid a pillow under her ass. Her rear entrance was now elevated, making it easier for Bill to penetrate. Carmella was ready for him as she relaxed her sphincter muscles and used her wide spread legs to raise her hips even more. As Bill pressed his large cock past the small opening, Carmella sighed with pleasure. There was no feeling like it. She never felt so possessed as she did when she was penetrated there. Liz's lips found hers again and Carmella greeted the woman's tongue with her own. Liz's hand was deep into Carmella's pussy as Bill thrust in and out of her ass. Liz broke off the kiss and whispered in Carmella's ear, "Come for me honey, let it flow." Carmella gave in to the pulses of pleasure floating through her. Her mouth opened and her hands gripped the sheets. Wave after wave of pleasure overwhelmed her as Liz caressed her pussy, peering intently into Carmella's face as she came.

Bill was still passionately stroking his cock in her rear, building to his own climax. Liz lifted her leg over Carmella's head, facing Bill, and placed her pussy on Carmella's mouth. "Suck my cunt, whore," she said hoarsely. She leaned between Carmella's upturned legs and placed her mouth on Bill's. They kissed passionately. "Don't come yet," she whispered to him. "Don't come yet."

Liz rocked her pelvis on Carmella's face and mouth. Carmella was reaching her second climax and sucked greedily on the crevasse that lay over her. Bill had slowed his stroke, waiting for Liz to catch up. Suddenly she moaned and called out to him, "Now, Bill, come now!" Liz's outburst triggered Bill's orgasm as he spurted his hot seed into Carmella's bowels. Their mouths pressed together, their tongues entwined passionately. Carmella came at the same time, clutching Liz's thighs and driving her face into Liz's crevasse.

Again the three collapsed into a jumble of arms and legs. No one spoke as they recovered their senses. This time it was Bill who stirred them from reverie. "We've got to get going Liz. The Count expects us for dinner."

"Oh," Liz sighed. I can't even think about dinner. I need a nap."

"Come on," Bill slapped her thigh lightly, "take a shower and you'll feel better."

So Bill and Liz rose from the bed and showered. Carmella waited patiently on her knees, her hands behind her. These strange, naïve Americans. Tomorrow or the next day they would be winging their way back to the States, to freedom. She would be an exciting memory for them. They had fucked a real sex slave.

The coupled dressed quickly after their shower. When they were ready to go, Liz knelt down next to Carmella and kissed her. "You were fantastic honey. Thanks." Then they walked out the door.

CHAPTER TEN

The former administrative assistant for a major New York stockbroker was on her knees, trembling. Her hands were locked behind her back and her skin was crisscrossed with marks of one or more severe lashings. Rashid had led her into Jeb's suite a few moments before and presented her. He had led her in on a leash and ordered her to her knees. She was gagged.

Jeb mulled over how exactly this was going to work out. This woman was supposed to be his new assistant. But she didn't look like she was ready to assist in anything. She certainly couldn't do any filing with her hands chained behind her back. And if she didn't stop crying, she would drive him mad. He decided to take a gentle approach.

"Stand up, Amy," he said softly. Tentatively, the woman rose from her knees. Jeb got up from his chair and walked over to her. He had read her resume, Amy Martelli, age 28. She had attended Fordham University and majored in business administration. She liked tennis and skiing. She was proficient in Word, Excel and a number of esoteric stock monitoring programs. She had worked on some rather large corporate mergers and was "looking to go to the next level."

She had reached a new level all right. And he was to blame. It was too late to do anything about it now. But just how was he going to work professionally with a naked woman wearing the accouterments of a slave girl? And when would she ever stop crying?

He reached behind the woman and unfastened her wrists. He loosened and removed the gag. "Have you had lunch?" he asked. Now that was a ridiculous thing to ask, he thought. But he had to break the ice somehow.

"N,no, master," she answered timidly.

She had been taught the basics of slavery: deference, politeness. "Then let me order us up something and we can get to know each other. Do you like fish?"

The girl was looking at him strangely, as if he were mad. Maybe he was.

"Y,yes, master."

"Good. I'll order some sole." He pointed to the dining table. "Have a seat."

Kneeling not far away was one of the ever present pleasure slaves. She too was looking at Jeb as if he was mad. But she knew better than to question him. "Slave," he said harshly, "go wait for me in the bedroom." The slave, fearing she had displeased him, rose and scurried away.

Jeb telephoned the kitchen and ordered two filets of sole. "Yes," he said, "two."

He knew the meals would be there in about fifteen minutes. Sole was on today's menu and so it would be ready to be cooked. He walked over to the table and sat opposite Amy.

He cleared his throat. "Ah, I know that this is difficult for you and, ah, I'm not sure how to approach this. I want you to believe me when I say that I had no knowledge that you were going to be brought here like this. I mean, I didn't want... it wasn't my decision...oh, you know what I'm trying to say." He was having a hard time finding the words.

The woman was still trembling, although she had stopped crying. "I, I don't know, master."

"Please, while you and I are alone I want you to call me Mr. Turner. Okay?"

"Y,yes, m,m, Mr. Turner." Jeb had just countermanded 48 hours of intensive training.

"But when anyone else is present, you should call me 'master'."

"Y,yes, master."

Jeb was having a hard time not looking at her breasts. They were shaking quite alluringly as the woman continued to tremble. The pale mounds were topped with dark red areolas and thin, hard nipples. Red lines crossed them, evidencing the cruel treatment she had received from Faisal. "I'll be that she has been fucked in ways that she couldn't have imagined two days ago," thought Jeb. The thing was that he wanted to fuck her too.

Seeing that his approach was getting nowhere, Jeb took a different tack. "Listen, Amy, and listen good. The only way things are going to change for you from now on is for the worst. I need someone to help me in my work. If you don't measure up, they'll get me someone else and you'll be shipped off to some whorehouse somewhere where you'll be fucking fifteen or twenty men a day until you wear out. So you better get a hold of yourself or I'll have to get rid of you."

This seemed to have an effect on the woman. Her eyes widened, an eagerness lit up in her face. "I'll do whatever you say, Mr. Turner, please don't send me away, please. I don't want to go back there. Please." She was holding back her tears, but barely.

"As long as you do what I say and cooperate with me there should be no problem. There's real work to do and I need it done right. I've got a lot of responsibility and I can't afford to let anyone fuck that up. Do you understand?"

"Yes, Mr. Turner, I understand."

"As long as you are working for me and as long as you give me your best efforts, you'll have the job."

"Thank you Mr. Turner. I'm sure I can help you. I know all about…"

"I know what you know," Jeb interrupted. "I just want your best."

"You'll get it Mr. Turner, I promise."

Jeb began to explain to Amy her new duties. She was to keep track of the research he did, type letters, and monitor certain market activity. She would field his calls, but, let there be no mistake, she was never to try to let anyone know anything about her status here or what had happened to her. Not even who she was.

Lunch was served. A slender, white-coated servant pushed a small cart into the room. Two silver domed plates were on it along with a bottle of Chablis and a pitcher of water. Jeb allowed the servant to place the plates in front of him and Amy. He shooed him out of the room before he could pour the wine.

"Wine is not for you," Jeb told Amy.

"Yes, Mr. Turner."

"Now eat. I can't assure you of this fine a meal every day. Protocol here would not allow it. But for today, you are my luncheon guest."

"Yes, Mr. Turner."

"Eat."

The two of them ate in silence. Amy was tentative with her fish. She apparently did not have much of an appetite. Jeb savored the tender fish served in a light mustard and onion sauce. The wine too was exquisite.

After he had supped to his content, Jeb addressed the pretty, naked, young woman again.

"There's one more thing I need to make clear to you."

"Yes, Mr. Turner."

Jeb fortified himself with a large gulp of wine. "Our working relationship here does not alter one basic fact," he explained. "As I said before, I did not bring you here, it was not what I had in mind."

"Yes, Mr. Turner."

"Let me be blunt," Jeb continued. "You are now a slave. As an attractive female slave, you will have certain, ah, other responsibilities." Jeb looked into Amy's face. She knew what he was talking about.

"You will provide me and, undoubtedly others, with whatever sexual services are demanded of you. You will devote as much earnestness to these duties as to any others. Do I make myself clear?"

Amy did not hesitate. "Perfectly clear, Mr. Turner." She had already learned that lesson.

"I want you to get up from the table, kneel at my feet and suck my cock," Jeb instructed her. "Later, after I've broken you in on some of the office procedures, we will go into my bedroom and I will fuck you. Is that clear?"

Amy replied in a determined, committed voice. "Perfectly clear, Mr. Turner."

She rose without further instruction and knelt at Jeb's feet. He turned his chair away from the table to give her access to his loins. Without hesitation, Amy undid his pants and extracted his flaccid cock. She leaned over and placed it between her lips. Jeb felt the gentle tugging on his tool as Amy swirled her tongue around it and sucked. The prick hardened rapidly under her eager efforts. She was no pleasure slave, but she had obviously had some experience and was wholly committed to her task.

Jeb closed his eyes and let the pleasure of this woman's mouth envelope him. It did not take long before he expelled a stream of viscous fluid into Amy's tender mouth. He panted rapidly as his throbbing meat sent signals of pleasure to his brain. When he was done, he stroked Amy's head and said, "Let's get to work."

* * * * * * * * * *

The Prince stood on the foredeck of his massive yacht as the sailors prepared to set out to sea. It had been another profitable night. There were twenty new slaves in the hold and $1.2 million dollars in cash in the safe. A very profitable night.

He was anchored off the shore of the Dalmatan Peninsula, officially in the waters of the new nation of Crotania, a breakaway republic of the former Soviet Union. Actually, a breakaway from a breakaway as the natives of this region had recently declared their independence. High level intervention from the United States and Russia was seeking to avert a new civil war in the region. Already, there had been skirmishes, raids, reprisals. And when the dogs of war were unleashed, men like the Prince always prospered.

Earlier that night, his ship had quietly anchored about a mile off of the Crotania coast. Lights were dimmed and he awaited the approach of a small craft. He did not have long to wait. A small motorboat came along side and two dark figures hustled aboard. The Prince met them in the reception room.

One of the men he knew. He had done business with him before. Through their dealings together slaves, heroin, guns and many other types of contraband had passed over his gunwale. And cash. Large quantities of cash.

"Sergi, it's good to see you, as always."

Sergi Krasjnavic, buyer, seller and broker of illicit goods, a frequenter of whorehouses, a cruel, vicious man.

"My Prince, I am your servant, as always. May I introduce General Pietr Blasic?"

The other man, dark and heavily bearded, nodded to the Prince. The Prince extended his hand and they shook. "Please," said the Prince, "have a seat." The Prince signaled for tea to be brought. The men sat down around his semicircular conference table.

Blasic spoke. "I hope I am not offending your hospitality, Prince, when I suggest that we make our conference brief. We have much business to do tonight and there is always the chance of a patrol boat, even here."

"Of course, General. Once we conclude our terms, we can commence the actual exchange of goods and cash. But I like to get the measure of the men I deal with and I've just met you."

Blasic nodded as if this were a thing understood between them.

"Please," continued the Prince, "give me a briefing on the current state of affairs. Are we talking about a long term relationship or will your men melt into the hills once a determined force is brought against you? Our prospective involvement with your cause is based on the assumption that we will continue to do business over an extended term."

Sergi remained silent. He was the broker here and it was best to let the principals speak for themselves.

Blasic shot back his tea and placed the cup on the table.

"I will not deceive you. I have 2500 men under arms at the present time. They are armed with what we could steal from our former rulers and many old, single bolt rifles. We have very few machine guns, almost no mortars and two tanks that we liberated from the other side, but not much gas." He paused to let the information sink in.

"But there are as many as 30,000 men who will assemble to our banner when we can arm them. We hold all the major passes between the capital and our lands. Winter is coming soon and offensive operations from the government will have to await the summer, since with the spring thaw, the roads will be all but impassable."

"So," the Prince observed, "you have time. But do you have the resources?"

"Ah yes, war and money," replied Blasic. "They are inseparable. Yes, we have the resources. Yesterday, my men seized a government convoy carrying $10 million dollars in gold. We have also seized the central bank in our region and many of its outlying branches. We are still assembling the cash. Mostly Euros, but many dollars, as you shall see tonight. For reasons of its own, the Russian Government, although publicly wringing its hands at the 'new tragedy in the Caucuses', is prepared to back us. I have with me a letter of credit for $500 million Rubles, equal to, I believe, $25 million dollars at current exchange rates." Blasic produced a document from his coat.

The Prince's bodyguard had stood close by during the conversation between the men. He bristled at Blasic's sudden movement to his pocket. He would have been dead in an instant if even a glint of metal had emerged from the coat.

Blasic handed the document to the Prince who examined it closely. "Of course, documents can be forged," the Prince said offhandedly.

The general slammed his rough, leathery hand on the table. "I swear on my mother's grave that this document is authentic!"

The Prince looked up at him. "Yes, I know it is," he said in a steely voice. "My agents have known of it for a week. If it was not authentic, my ship would not be sitting within gunshot of your so-called capital city."

"I apologize for my outburst," Blasic said in a low tone. "We have been fighting for days without rest. Only yesterday did we subdue the last village on our side of the mountains. Many have died. I know, with all due respect, that you are a businessman. But our cause burns hot in my blood."

"I can see that it does," replied the Prince. "And I can see that your cause is led by a man of substance and honesty. That is what I came here to find out. I am very satisfied. Let's get down to business."

The general outlined his hopes for equipment and resources. The Prince outlined costs and possible delivery dates. Agreement was reached quickly.

"I am prepared to turn over a little over a million dollars tonight in good faith," Blasic said.

"And I," replied the Prince, "have a shipment of 500 automatic rifles, 300,000 rounds of ammunition, seven heavy mortars, some uniforms, boots and other necessities. Also, I understand that a selection has been made from your female prisoners and that twenty, let us say, guests, will be delivered to my boat tonight."

"Yes, yes, Sergi had made a selection for you. I'll be frank, my Prince," Blasic answered. "I would have had them all shot were it not for your particular interest. My people have suffered depredations from the fathers and husbands of these whores for many years. We are purging our land of these people. There will be many more, I can promise you."

"I will hold you to that promise," replied the Prince.

"I expect that you will," Blasic said. "I will order my boats to come aside your vessel so that the goods can be exchanged. If you will now permit me, I will return ashore in my motorboat."

The men nodded, stood and all shook hands.

It took the better part of an hour for the 'goods' to be exchanged. The first barge came alongside almost at once. The Prince's men manhandled the crates from below decks as the barge disgorged ten beautiful bound and gagged young women to the yacht's deck. A small suitcase was delivered to Sergi, who had remained on board. A quick check of its contents revealed $600,000.

"I see that your general is not taking any chances," the Prince remarked to Sergi.

"Yes," Sergi replied, "and I am sure he will check every crate when it comes ashore before sending the next half of the money and women. He has to be careful."

"Oh, yes, I am sure that he does. But he will find it all in order. But let me take a look at the first boatload of our new guests," the Prince said.

The two men walked amidships where the ten women were kneeling on the deck. They had been roped together to prevent any one of them from trying to jump over the side. Now that they had been delivered, their security was the Prince's responsibility.

The women were all young, but mature, between the ages of 18 and 21. They all shared a frightened, wide-eyed look as they tried to divine what fate had in store for them. They had been separated from their mothers and sisters earlier. It did not take much of an imagination to realize that they, the prettiest and youngest of the lot, had been singled out for that very reason. They had expected to be raped. The fact that they had not been was mystifying. And now, they had been delivered to this boat in the middle of the night. To the smartest of them, certainly, the fact that large crates were being lowered to the deck of the boat they had just left suggested some form of quid pro quo.

The Prince walked among the group of huddling, young women. They were mostly raven haired, with two blonds and one auburn haired girl. They were dressed in the clothes they had been seized in, mostly blouses and skirts. Two were wearing what seemed to be fashionable, tight blue jeans. They did not seem damaged, although the blouse of one had been torn open and a delicate, white, lacey bra could be seen holding in two porcelain white globes.

Other than being beautiful and shapely, their physical attributes were varied. Large breasts predominated, as would be expected. But others had breasts of moderate to even small size. One of the girls was diminutive in stature and two seemed rather tall, although from a kneeling position it was hard to tell. The Prince yearned to inspect them more thoroughly, but knew it best to await the completion of the exchange and the open sea.

It was a windy, overcast night, and the darkness was perfect for the accomplishment of clandestine activity. Several of the girls had quite long hair, and the gusting breezes tossed their manes about wildly. None of the girls was dressed for the cold and the sharp, early winter air caused them to huddle together for warmth. They all watched the Prince apprehensively as he took his time in examining them. His refined dress and dignified carriage was in sharp contrast to the rough men who had captured and guarded them up to now.

The Prince watched as, one by one, the second consignment of girls was brought aboard. Their hands were bound behind them by rough, thick ropes and their mouths were split open by tightly tied cloths. They seemed too frightened to cry.

A soon as the last crate was taken overboard and the last girl pressed to her knees and coffled to the others, the Prince gave orders to prepare to get underway. The girls were hustled below decks, crying and wailing as they were roughly handled by the crew. Sergi and the Prince retired to the reception room to count the second suitcase of cash. It was all there.

Sergi snapped the suitcase shut and smiled. Things had not been this good since the Bosnian war. There he had done business with all sides and had graduated from a mere henchman to the leader of a gang of grim cutthroats. His craftiness and ruthlessness had taken him to the top of the pyramid. His scarred cheek was testimony to the brute force necessary to such a climb.

"Just like the good old days," he said to the Prince.

"Yes, Sergi, another gift from the God of War," the Prince replied.

"I have a special gift for you, Prince. If you will allow me a few moments…"

"A gift?"

"Yes, in anticipation of the fruitfulness of our coming endeavors," Sergi answered. "And in anticipation of certain requests."

The Prince laughed. "In my country," he responded, "it is said to look closely in the eyes of the gift giver."

Sergi laughed in response. "That is good advice. But first look at the gift, eh?"

"I am at your mercy, Sergi. Please don't keep me in suspense."

Sergi hustled off. About ten minutes later he reappeared. He had in tow a smartly dressed, middle-aged woman. She had black hair, a finely sculpted face. She was bound and gagged in the same manner as the young girls who had been previously been brought on deck. She was in her early forties and the refinement of her clothes and her well-preserved features bespoke wealth and privilege.

"Please meet Madam Kristina Paralova, the wife, or should I say widow, of the former governor of this province," Sergi said to the Prince.

The Prince laughed. "I am honored, Mrs. Paralova."

Sergi stood away from the comely woman so that the Prince could appreciate her charms. She was attractive, but hardly slave stock. She might be an interesting diversion from the steady diet of firm, youthful flesh, but not a female who presented any great potential profit. Her eyes blazed with hatred.

"A lovely creature, Sergi," said the Prince politely. "I am sure that I can find some use for her...."

"But Prince," Sergi interrupted, "there is more."

He signaled to the doorway and three pretty, young women were led into the room. They were astoundingly beautiful. They were dressed in chic, tightly fitted skirts and designer blouses. Their eyes were bright, intense. "Ah," the Prince said, surprised, "there is more?"

"Your Highness," Sergi said, "let me introduce Katya Paralova, Nadia Paralova and Nadine Paralova, the three beautiful daughters of Mrs. Kristina Paralova, at your service."

The Prince was overjoyed. "Sergi, you overwhelm me! A trio of sisters, and their mother too! What can I say? I am in your debt."

"I had hoped that you would be pleased," Sergi said.

"Pleased? My mind reels!" The Prince stepped toward the young women. Sensing his malicious intent, the three sisters all cringed and tried to shy away from him. However, their arms were held tightly by the sailors who had led them into the room. Their faces were so similar they could be triplets. Black hair, pale skin, shapely breasts that pushed out from beneath their blouses. They also shared an indescribable refinement that bespoke pampered luxury, finishing schools and genteel living. Their mouths were pulled back in strange grimaces by the rudimentary gags. Like the other women who had been brought aboard, they were barefoot, their ankles linked by a short rope.

"Sergi, Sergi, Sergi," the Prince exclaimed, "you are a magician. I accept you gift with profound appreciation." He paused and looked at Sergi. "And what is your price?"

"Not a price, my Prince, a request."

"And?"

"With this new endeavor, I will be at the point where I am considering retirement, or at least partial retirement. I would like to settle in Calipha and I know that that is only possible if I have an influential sponsor."

"Sergi, assuming you can meet the financial requirements, you will have my blessing," the Prince replied.

"And there is one more thing." Sergi continued.

The Prince chuckled, "There is always one more thing."

"Yes," Sergi confirmed, "there is always one more thing. But this thing is small and inconsequential. There is a slave in your House of Pleasure, her name is Carmella."

"Carmella?" the Prince inquired.

"Yes, Carmella. She is currently serving, on my information, as an upstairs girl. I will not try and mislead you, she is a very comely wench and a fine whore. I would like to buy her contract from you."

"Carmella, eh," the Prince mused. He knew that name. "An upstairs girl?" he inquired. "How long has she been serving there?"

"I believe that she has been serving you for only a few months."

"You know our policy is to let upstairs girls serve as long as possible before we sell their contracts. After all we have a substantial investment in them."

"I realize that, my Prince, but…"

"And why is this particular whore of such concern to you?" the Prince interrupted.

"The best way I can express it is to say that she brings out the fire in me. I can think only of tormenting her and using her. I don't know why, but the little cunt has bewitched me."

"Ahhhhhhh," the Prince responded. "This I understand." There had been a few over the years who had bewitched him. Eventually they had been used up, but not until he had scaled new heights of delight with each of them.

"I will give this great thought, Sergi," the Prince announced. "You have been a good business associate for many years. Hundreds of comely females owe their bondage to your efforts and you have made me a great deal of money. I do not take your request lightly and will give it careful consideration."

"That is all I ask, my Prince"

And so the Prince stood on the foredeck, mulling over Sergi's request. Of course he knew Carmella. He remembered fondly the little drink they had shared in his casino a few short months ago. She was a lovely creature. It had been his telephone call to the security police that had alerted them to her escape attempt. After all, her lover had just robbed him of $40,000. No one stole from him, no one!

But he did have plans for Carmella. It had taken some effort to lure her lover back into the country. He knew full well the charade Jeb was conducting and it amused him to have him repay his debt many times over by managing his financial affairs, at least those he had allowed him to have knowledge of. And it had amused him to watch closely as Jeb had, step by step, been corrupted from his Western ideals. He had seen the lust in Jeb's eyes as he witnessed the whipping of poor Vicki. His pleasure slaves had all reported their experiences with him in great detail. He had not decided how, in the end, he would deal with Jeb. After all, he was entitled to his revenge. Perhaps knowing that his lover had been sold to one of the cruelest men the Prince had ever known would be an appropriate punishment.

CHAPTER ELEVEN

The Prince felt the ship begin to move and he took himself back to the reception room. Calipha was several days away, and he had some new toys to play with. And there were the twenty comely cunts to assess.

Returning to the reception room, the Prince took in the sight of the four Paralova women, bound and gagged and awaiting his pleasure. He had ordered them hooded and hog-tied. He had left the crude bindings that General Blasic's men had affixed in place. He would deal with them later.

He proceeded below decks to the slave quarters. Normally, the ship carried a complement of twelve pleasure slaves. Each one was allotted a small cage for sleeping purposes. There were three extra cages in case of acquisitions during a voyage. Anticipating the delivery of twenty new females, he had brought only five pleasure slaves with him. That left ten cages for twenty women. They would be cramped, but they would have to make do.

The Prince had also brought along a staff of the huge, jet black, Sudanese guards he used to control and intimidate slaves at his mansion and in the working areas of the House of Adeem. They were, as a group, tall and well built. Tribal customs had scared their faces, giving them a demonic look. Their fierce visages together with the strong well muscled bodies created an ambiance of fear for the women. And the customers liked the irony of these jet black, scarred men controlling beautiful, mostly white, female slaves.

The men were fiercely loyal and well disciplined. They were rewarded well, too. Many a demoted pleasure slave had spent time in service in their barracks. Several of these girls were now in the crew's area, available to the crew and the guards. He always brought a few second rank slaves on these voyages. The staff needed some outlet for their lusts, as they were daily confronted with the pulchritude of the pleasure slaves reserved for the Prince, the boat's officers and the guests.

He usually had two or three of the Sudanese guards aboard during his voyages, to control the twelve sublime females he brought for his daily pleasure. But those slaves were all well trained and rebellion was a word that had been taken from their vocabulary. These new slaves would be desperate, frightened creatures. They needed to be cowed right from the start. For this purpose he brought an extra six of these Sudanese guards along with him to help regulate and control the new slaves. They would tend to be unruly until taught discipline through a taste or two of the whip. The large, fierce looking, black warriors would strike fear into the women.

The frightened, disorientated, young women were waiting for the Prince's appearance in the assembly area outside the slave sleeping quarters. They had all been untied and they stood there, hands on their heads, legs spread. Their gags had been removed, but silence had been enforced strictly by the guard's canes.

Ngumo was the Captain of the guards and the Prince's chief enforcer aboard. Ngumo slapped his cane against the cabin's steel wall making a loud abrasive clanging noise. The women, standing in four rows of five, elbow to elbow, snapped to attention. The Prince took in the vision of the twenty comely females who were about to learn their first lessons of slavery. "Just like the good old days," Sergi had said. Quite right. If the civil war lasted a year, he could harvest at least three hundred new slaves, three hundred women who would learn the lessons of the lash and the chain. He wouldn't take more than that, and he would take only the best. He couldn't afford to have a glut on the market. During the Bosnian years the price of a white slave woman had fallen miserably due to the hundreds of Croat, Serb, Bosnian and other ethnic group women who had fallen into bondage. He had traded with them all during that war. He got Bosnians and Croats from the Serbs, Serbs and Croats from the Bosnians and Bosnians and Serbs from the Croats. From time to time he dealt with freebooters, gangs of men, like Sergi's, who owed allegiance to no cause or faith other than greed and lust.

The only problem had been the Bosnian women who were mostly Moslems. He was forbidden to enslave Moslem women and it was often difficult to get them to renounce their faith so that they could then be enslaved. Faith was a funny thing and there were a few of those girls who had to be finally thrown over the side, having gotten their wish of death before dishonor. The demonstration of tossing over board a naked, chained woman, weighted down with cement blocks was usually enough to get the rest to put aside their qualms. But these new women were all Christians. And the women he would be able to harvest from the other side would be Christians too. Different sects of course, but all freely enslaveable.

The women all looked at the Prince apprehensively. He was clearly in command here. He had a regal bearing that was unmistakable and, besides, all the men, even the savage looking blacks, paid deference to him. He was clearly the person who was in control of their fates.

The Prince addressed the women in a stern, yet unhostile tone. "Is there anyone among you who can speak English?" he asked. He, of course, did not speak the particular Slavic tongue spoken by these women. The women looked around at each other. Who would dare step forward? Well, the one who hoped to ease her own fate by obeisance to her captors, the one who would serve as the Judas goat for them all.

A pretty little black haired girl, wearing a long, flowing skirt and a peasant blouse spoke up. "I speak English," she said in a small, heavily accented voice.

"Come forward, please," the Prince requested.

Hesitatingly, the girl walked up to the front of the assemblage of frightened young women and presented herself to the Prince. The Prince nodded to Ngumo who quickly and deftly grabbed her by the hair and gave her four sharp slaps across her face. The petit woman was shocked at the assault. She cried out in pain and struggled to avoid the blows. Gasps of alarm could be heard from the other women.

Ngumo, still holding the young woman by her hair turned her to face the Prince. He spoke to her in a low voice.

"You will translate exactly what I say. And you will do exactly as I command. Is that clear?"

"Yes! Yes!" the girl sputtered. "Please don't hit me!"

"Very well. Now tell the women what I say," the Prince commanded. He had a little speech prepared. The tearful and trembling girl translated his words as he paused between simple, short passages.

"My name is Prince Harim Adeem Baroof. You have been taken aboard my yacht and are now my prisoners. There are some very basic rules here." He paused to let the trembling young girl next to him translate.

"Those rules are that you will remain silent at all times and you will obey all of the orders given to you. Failure to obey these rules will result in painful punishment." He nodded again to Ngumo. The guard signaled to two of his compatriots who stepped up and grabbed a woman at random from the crowd. She was wearing a Western style skirt and a plain white blouse. She had long brown hair and gentle features. She struggled and called out some words in her native tongue as she was dragged to the front of the room.

While one of the guards held her hands above her head, the other proceeded to rip her blouse and bra from her body. She screamed as she was being manhandled. Murmurs of outrage mixed with terror rose from the other captive females.

The guards strapped the wrists of the now half naked woman to a ring about six feet off of the deck. Her skin was smooth and flawless. Her breasts swung free, twin peaks of snow-white flesh. Once her hands were tied above her, she was facing the bulkhead, tears in her eyes, trying to pull her shoulders and arms together to hide her pretty tits from view. Her face was a mixture of hate and fear. She cried out several harsh words in her own language and then switched to English, "Pigs, swine, I curse you!" She spit at the Prince. "You are animals! God curse you all!"

"Good," the Prince thought. "They picked out the right one."

The other women broke formation and started yelling epithets at the Prince and the guards. Several slashing blows of the guard's canes drove them back. And then Ngumo produced a long, single lashed whip. He swung it back and then forwards. A loud crack resounded in the room, even above the emboldened voices of the rebellious women. They all turned to see what the noise was, suddenly silenced. The bound woman let out a loud, lamenting cry. "Ohhhhhhhhhhhhh!"

"Crack!" A second blow fell, raising immediately a second bright red, angry welt on her back. She screamed. The other women, now cowed, cringed at the sound of the whip and the woman's painful cries. Another snap of the whip, "Crack!" The tormented woman began to cry out in Slavic and in English. "Please, stop, I beg of you, please stop!"

Another blow fell, and another. The woman now was hysterical. One of the guards spun her body around making her tits available for whipping. Realizing what was to come, the woman pleaded and begged all the harder. "Please, I'll do anything! I'm sorry, I'm sorry, please forgive me! Oh, please don't whip my breasts, please!"

The Prince raised a hand and Ngumo hesitated. He addressed the trembling, tearful woman. "What is your name?" he asked.

She was taken aback by the question, but after only a moment's hesitation said, "Lara."

"Lara, I want you to apologize to me."

The crowd of women was silent, staring at the spectacle of the helpless beauty.

"I, I'm sorry," the girl said softly, tearfully.

"No," said the Prince. "You must speak loudly so that everyone can hear. And you must say, 'I am sorry, master.'" He turned to the slight framed girl who was serving as his translator. "You will tell them what she says, word for word." His voice was a stern command. The translator stirred from her shock and nodded.

The bound woman was crying, sobbing. She looked up at the Prince, realizing the import of the words. She was to acknowledge his ownership of her, his mastery, her enslavement. Her eyes shifted to Ngumo and his whip. She did not want more of that. Eventually, she would do anything they wanted to avoid pain anyway. It had taken her all of one minute to realize that, one minute to shatter her conceptions of who she was, to destroy her arrogance and courage. She looked back at the Prince. He was staring at her expectantly.

The slave called out loudly, "I am sorry, master!" Her words were translated for the other, now subdued women.

"You are forgiven," the Prince said softly. The guards unloosened her wrists from the ring. Her knees buckled as she tried to stand, and she had to be supported by the guards while she gained her composure. Suddenly, realizing that her breasts were bare for all to see, she tried to pull her arms free to cover them.

"No, no, no," said the Prince, speaking as one would to a child. "You mustn't hide your breasts. Put your arms on your head." The last words were spoken sternly. The girl immediately did what she was told. The crowd of women had lowered their arms during the commotion, but it only took a gentle prodding of the guards' canes to get them back in position.

"Step closer, child," the Prince said to Lara. She took tentative steps towards him until she was about two feet away. She was to the side of the room, to the left of the Prince. Her profile was presented to the other women. The Prince reached out a hand and stroked the side of her left breast so that all could see. Lara shuddered at his touch, but did not flinch. Her raised arms uplifted her breasts, two delicate, white globes, firm and soft. Her nipples were hard with fear.

"You have beautiful breasts, Lara. I can see why you wanted to protect them," the Prince said. He looked at her expectantly. Lara looked back, uncertain as to what he wanted. There was a long pause and she realized what the Prince was waiting for.

"Thank you, master," she said, her voice a nervous whisper.

She did not have to speak loud for the small crowd of young women to understand what was happening. Lara had been tamed by five strokes of a whip. This feisty, brave compatriot of theirs had surrendered abjectly to the will of this harsh and cruel man. The lesson had been learned. What chance did they have to oppose his will?

The Prince smiled at the deference of this delectable female. "It did not take much," he thought.

"Lara, please take off the rest of your clothes," the Prince said politely.

Lara was startled at the request. To undress in front of these men and all of these women! Since she was ten, not even her mother had seen her naked. She knew she had no choice. She looked quickly at Ngumo and the whip he still had in his hands. She looked at the strange looking, callous black men who stood near him. They would strip her anyway and she would suffer. She had to obey.

Slowly, Lara brought her arms down from her head to her waist. She struggled momentarily at the clasp at the front of her skirt, her hands sweaty with fear. The clasp was released and she hesitated before lowering the skirt to the floor. She closed her eyes and pushed the waistband down, letting the long, knee length skirt follow it past her knees, her ankles and then over her feet.

She held the skirt in her hands, not knowing what to do with it. She was wearing sheer, lacy panties, arched highly at her thighs. Her brown bush could be easily discerned at her front. She tried to hide it with the skirt, but the Prince removed it from her hands. With a sharp sob, she hooked her hands in the elastic of her panties and pulled them to her feet and then stepped out of them.

Her hips were wide, her calves and thighs well toned and defined. The Prince signaled her to replace her hands on her head and she did so. She was a marvelous sight, a presage of the beauty the Prince expected from all of the women. Sergi had a master's eye for beauteous flesh.

The Prince ordered her to turn around so that he could see her ass. It was deliciously rounded and firm. Her back bore the angry welts produced by her whipping, but was otherwise unmarred. The Prince ran his hands down her sides and over her hips and ass, enjoying the feel of her. He reached around her and cupped her breasts, kneading them and pinching the nipples.

All of this was on view to the other women. Their fate was being spelled out to them through the person of Lara. Fear, shame and sorrow spread through them as they anticipated their turn at being stripped and subjected to the Prince's grossly indecent caresses.

Ngumo had reached into a carton on the deck nearby and produced a leather belt. He handed it to the Prince who, after turning Lara back to face him, circled it around her waist. He locked it in place and then guided Lara's hands, one after the other, to her hips where they were confined in bracelets affixed to the belt. Lara's face contorted with shame and fear as she tested the bindings on her wrists. While she was discovering the unforgiving nature of her new bonds, Ngumo produced from another carton a smaller belt with a large protruding wedge of leather. It was a gag, designed to fill a victim's mouth, preventing all but the most violent moans and cries to escape. Opposite the gag, on the other side, was a wide, curved, leather panel, meant to shield the mouth and lips, rendering the face almost featureless. It was stamped with a gold embossed number.

The Prince presented the gag to Lara. She stared at it, realizing its purpose. She began to whine.

"No, please do not do this. I'll be quiet, please. I couldn't stand it, please!"

"Now Lara, you must open your mouth," the Prince said almost sweetly. "We don't want any trouble, do we?"

Lara was too overcome to reply, but she opened her mouth, slightly, at first, but then widely as the gag was shoved home by the Prince. He handed off the straps to Ngumo who fastened them behind the forlorn woman's head.

Lara, who almost certainly had never been gagged before, sagged slightly, on the verge of fainting. Two guards alertly grabbed her elbows and held her up.

There was a ring embedded in the outer part of the gag, in the middle of the sheath that covered almost all of the lower face. The Prince crooked his finger into it and pulled Lara closer to him. He leaned over and whispered something in her ear. Lara cringed noticeably, a low groan escaping from her gag. Before they reached Calipha, she would serve the Prince's pleasure.

The Prince had been accompanied by two of his diminutive brown skinned servants when he entered the assembly area outside the slave quarters. One of them took hold of Lara's arm and began to lead her away through the door that led to the cages which would be the home of these unfortunate women for the next few days. As he did, the Prince leaned over to the other servant, who was holding a clipboard and whispered, "Lara, tag number 212, rating, 8.5." Lara had been graded for her desirability.

One by one, the other women were led up to the Prince. He needed no translation for his order for them to strip.

Resistance was out of the question. The small girl who had been selected as the Prince's voice to those who did not speak English called out his commands as he had them turn and display themselves. Only two girls demonstrated any real reluctance to disobey orders. All of the others, remembering the shocking sight of Lara's whipping, obeyed unreservedly. The two who hesitated were motivated by quick blows from Ngumo's cane.

The young women were all sizes and shapes, but, almost without exception, the pinnacle of female physical beauty. The Prince, after his initial inspection of each new slave, called out a number to his aide: 8, 9, 8.5, 9.5. Only one merited a ten.

She was a tall, thin, longhaired blonde. Her skin was as pale as ivory, almost translucent. Her face was ethereal, haunting. She answered the Prince's questions in a sweet, sonorous, but tremulous voice. She had long, graceful legs and narrow, almost boy-like hips. Her breasts were milky white, large for her slender body. She was thin, but not boney, with ample, firm flesh. Her name was Alisha. She was 21. "No," she replied meekly to the Prince's indecent inquiry as to whether she was a virgin. She had no English. The Prince was intrigued by her beauty and lingered over her, examining her minutely. He had resisted any overtly sexual ministrations with the others, aside from stroking their breasts, and, perhaps, pinching their nipples. But this, he could not resist.

Once she had been bound and gagged, he drew Alisha closer. He nudged her thighs apart and covered her sex with his hand. Her pubic hair was thin, but long. Her cunt was moist at his touch. The Prince entered her pussy with his hand, reveling in the softness within. After only a few strokes, she began to breathe deeply, her eyes to flutter. Her small nipples had engorged and were pointed and hard. Her body began to sway as the Prince rubbed the nub at the apex of her sex.

"Yes," the Prince thought, "she is a 10. A keeper."

He released her before she could climax. He waved his wet hand under her nose so that she could smell the odor of her own arousal. She stiffened at the musty aroma, her eyes now wide, expressive of her dismay at her own lasciviousness.

"She's to have a solitary cell," the Prince commanded the servant who had been escorting the women to their crowded berths. He caressed her nipples once more before she was taken away.

Ultimately, there was left only the small, obsequious translator. She was now alone in the company of these predatory men. She had known, once the evaluation process began, that she would be last. That seemed like a good thing. She realized now, however, that the comfort of the sympathy of her fellow prisoners was to be denied her. And by being last, she would almost certainly be the repository for the steady, inexorable build up of the lust of the Prince and the other strange, fearsome men.

The girl began to cry. She had seen the humiliation of the other women, the callousness with which they had been handled. This was now to be her fate. Without a word from the Prince, she began to disrobe. She removed her blouse revealing heavy, almost pendulous breasts. She shed her skirt and panties quickly, tossing them into the large pile of female clothing that had amassed in the corner of the room. Attempting to disguise her fear, she stood proudly before the Prince. She jutted out her breasts and spread her thighs. She desperately wanted to be considered special by this heartless man. Perhaps she could avoid some of the pain and hardship that presaged to be the fate of the other women.

The girl had long, black hair, seemingly longer due to the shortness of her stature. Her nipples were a dark red, her areolas wide, her nipples thick and appetizing. Her facial features were small, almost child-like. She was trembling in spite of her resolve to be fearless and composed.

"Ah, my dear," the Prince said to her, "thank you for your valuable services here tonight."

The girl did not hesitate in answering, "You're welcome, master."

"Please turn around so that I can see your ass." The Prince knew what game she was playing and was determined to let her debase herself. The girl turned around and, keeping her hands on her head, displayed her firm, well-rounded posterior to the Prince. The other men, the hulking, black monsters, who had acted as the Prince's enforcers, circled around her. She began to sweat with fear. One of the guards had his hand inside his belt, stroking his cock.

"Please, my dear, bend over and grab your ankles," the Prince requested.

None of the other girls had been asked to do this and the petit woman felt a knot in her stomach. She was no virgin. But her couplings had been with a single partner, an older man who had treasured her appealing body, had treated her with kindness. One thing she knew for certain, these men were not kind.

The frightened young woman bent over and stretched her arms as long as they could go. She was more than mortified as her lovely pussy and the wrinkled opening to her ass were now prominently displayed. She felt a hand between her thighs, which were still tightly together. "Spread your legs, slave," the Prince said.

Now it had been said, what she had been hoping against hope was not true. These men were enslaving her! She and the others were being taken god knew where to become whores of the lowest kind. They would have no rights, no say in what happened to them. "Please sir," she managed to say as she obeyed the Prince's command, "I don't want to be a slave." Her voice was forlorn, weak, without conviction. She knew it was useless to plead.

The Prince rubbed the soft lips of her quim from behind. "But you were born to be a slave, my little whore," he told her. "It was your destiny."

The girl could only see the leather clad feet of the men who surrounded her. She knew that they were awaiting only a signal from this man, their leader, before they would heartlessly begin to ravage her. Her pussy was moist now, the lips of its entrance soft and flushed. She had a passionate nature, and the Prince's hand was stoking her lust against her will. She felt him pinch lightly her little pleasure bud and she moaned. There was laughter all around her.

"You have not told me your name, pretty one," the Prince said as he delved deeper into her burning hole.

Fear and the build up of her desire made it hard to speak. "M,Maria. My name is Maria," she finally answered.

"That's a pretty name, Maria," the Prince taunted her. "These men are going to fuck you now, Maria, and, when they're done, they are going to bind and gag you and put you in a cage with your friends. Is that all right with you Maria?"

Never had anything been less all right with her. The strange surroundings, this vault of steel walls and floors, the harsh lighting, the echoes of their voices in the now almost empty room, had an eerie effect. It was both unreal and horribly real at the same time. It was like a nightmare, but she had never been more awake.

She dared not answer no. She remembered well the sound of the whip as it had torn into the first woman's body. She did no want to be whipped. She was sure she would be raped anyway. Timidly, she uttered a soft, "Yes."

"Yes, what Maria?" the Prince asked.

"Yes, master," the girl replied tearfully.

"Do your best for my men, Maria. Give them all a good fuck. And they may want you to suck their pricks, Maria. Do you know how to suck a prick, Maria?"

Maria was panting now as the Prince rubbed her pussy in earnest, massaging the very tip, running his fingers inside and out of her hot sheath. She did not want to answer. But she knew she must. "Yes, master."

"Good. Then you wouldn't mind sucking a few hard, black cocks, would you?"

"No, master."

"Have you ever had a black cock in your mouth Maria?" the Prince continued, tauntingly.

"No, master." The woman's voice was almost lost as she began to moan violently. "No, not here," she thought. "Not in front of these cruel men."

But she was no longer master of her body and she began to convulse with unwanted pleasure. "Ah, ah, ah!" she cried as her cunt throbbed. She was humping back at the Prince's hand now, uncaring of the obscene display of her body. Her tits rocked back and forth lewdly as the five guards watched with glee and lust. She was a pretty one. They all anticipated the squeeze of her tight, young pussy on their cocks.

The Prince relented from his abuse of her sex. He wiped his hand on her ass. "Enjoy your fucking, Maria, I'll see you tomorrow, o.k.?"

Maria could hardly stand. Reflexively, she uttered a low, "Yes, master."

"I'm going to fuck you and then I'm going to whip you. Okay, Maria?"

Maria started a low wail. She was going to be whipped! "Oh, please don't whip me master, please!"

The Prince nodded to Ngumo, who of course would be first. Ngumo already had his thick, black cock out of his pants. The Prince watched as he shoved it home into the already well lubricated gash between Maria's legs. She uttered a cry of surprise and tried to stand, but another of the guards grabbed her shoulders and forced her down, bent in two. He slipped his cock into her reluctantly obedient mouth. The Prince watched for a moment, the black cocks driving in and out of the white girl's flesh. Then he left.

CHAPTER TWELVE

As the Prince's yacht rounded the point that lay leeward of Calipha Bay, he was sitting in a lounge chair under the yellow awning amidships. There was a pleasant breeze and he allowed himself to admire the glint of the sun off of the water. He had had a marvelous night. The Paralova girls were enchantingly beautiful. And the mother, a hellcat. He had not decided yet whether he would keep them or sell them on. Three sisters and a mother would bring a wondrous price. But the enjoyment in the debasement of these innocent girls, protected in the womb of their strict Christian family, the favored and pampered children of wealth, would also be great. The youngest, Katya, was just over eighteen, the oldest, Nadia, just under 22. Nadine was 20. And all virgins. He had checked for himself.

The night he had acquired them he had returned to the reception room after watching Maria roundly fucked by two of his Sudanese guards. When he left, she had been shifted to her knees and a stiff, black cock was mashed between her rear cheeks. He had seen Maria that next morning and had administered the promised fuck and lashing. She had screamed and begged piteously. He had sent her astern this morning for the delight of the sailors as they approached their home port.

But the Paralovas, ah, these were women. That first night, after returning from below decks, he had ordered the women unhooded and their legs released. His servants stood them all up in the center of the room. The mother,

Kristina, stood there proudly, her eyes like daggers. The Prince had her gag removed.

She lit into him immediately. "I demand to be set free! I am the wife of a provincial governor. My father is the chief advisor to the Premier! You have no right to hold us here!" Her chest heaved as she boiled over with indignation. "And my daughters, how dare you treat them this way! Untie us immediately!"

The Prince laughed and clapped his hands at the bravura performance. "Well, done Madam Paralova. Well done. But you see, it doesn't please me to let you go. In fact, I'm afraid that you are going to be greatly displeased at what the future holds in store for you and your beautiful daughters."

"Don't you touch my daughters, you scum," the enraged woman cried.

"Not yet, Madam Paralova. First I am going to make a little demonstration for them of you. Then I am going to strip them and let you lick their pretty little cunts with my cock up your ass. But you will have to beg me first."

The prim, haughty woman leaned over and spit in the Prince's face. "I'll die first," she cried.

"Hang her in the frame," the Prince ordered as he wiped her spittle from his face. Two of the Prince's guards sprung into action. They dragged the woman from the floor to the steel frame at the rear of the reception room. She was quickly mounted, her arms and legs akimbo, hanging by her wrists. While she was still struggling, the Prince pressed a ball gag into her mouth and locked it behind her head.

"Strip her!" he ordered. The two tall black men began to rip her clothes from her. She struggled vainly as first her skirt and then her blouse were rent asunder. She was wearing lacy, but modest white panties and a dainty bra that lifted her breasts upwards, her nipples peaking over the tops. Soon they were gone and she faced her tormentor, naked.

She was still firm and taut, despite her middle age, and her breasts had aged well. They were round and firm, with a slight droop, inevitable under the circumstances.

The Prince turned to the three young girls who had just witnessed the first stages of their mother's debasement. They had heard the threats. If their mother was powerless to oppose this man, what resistance could they offer?

"Unfasten their bindings. Leave them gagged," the Prince ordered. The arms of the three pretty females were freed. Their mouths were still pulled open by the cloth bindings that had been tied around their heads. They looked at the Prince with fear.

He had been handed a short whip by one of the servants. "Strip," he ordered. He did not know if they spoke English or not, but his meaning was clear enough.

Frantically, the three girls began to disrobe. They were all crying and bumped against each other in their haste to remove their clothing. Unlike their mother, their underclothes were daring and provocative. Two, Katya and Nadia, the youngest and oldest, wearing thin, revealing thongs and half bras, in matching pastel colors. The middle one, Nadine, was wearing a sheer, silk chemise over tiny silk panties that rode high on her hips. It was all off quickly, joining the pile of outer clothing that had gathered at their feet. One of the servants stepped over and removed the clothes. They would have no further need for them.

The girls stood huddled together, expectantly. Their bodies were delicately beautiful, soft skin, small, white breasts. They were as similar in appearance as three sisters could be without being triplets. The Prince had their arms rebound, this time in front of them. Katya, the youngest, started to sob as her hands were joined by one of the large, black guards. Mama was struggling wildly in the frame, vainly and loudly protesting, through her gag, her daughters' treatment.

The girls' hands were then bound to chains from the ceiling and they were stretched to their full heights. The Prince examined them appreciatively. They were a treasure. Their little brown bushes faintly disguised their inviting pussies. The tears streaming down their faces gave them an alluring vulnerability. They were all posed so that they would have a clear view of their mother's torment and their eyes darted from the whip that the Prince was playfully swinging in his hands to their mother's struggling form.

Turning quickly, the Prince struck the mother full force with the whip across her stomach. She stiffened with the pain and screeched from behind her gag. Silently, remorselessly, he flailed her body as she danced helplessly in the air. The frame was on wheels and so he was able to have her turned around so the daughters could watch as he crisscrossed her back and the rear of her thighs with stripes.

The whip was then handed to one of the guards, who continued the mother's abuse as the Prince stepped off to take a refreshment. Every inch of the mother's body was mauled by the biting lashes of the many thonged whip. The Prince had the guard pause as he approached the moaning, crying woman.

"We have just begun, Madam Paralova. In a little while we will begin again, but this time with the crop." The woman was sagging in her bonds. She had a defeated look and the Prince was sure that, if given the opportunity, she would beg for release, promise anything. But she wasn't quite ready to <u>do</u> anything, to debase herself and her children at his command and for his pleasure. That would come later, when the torment had driven her past all endurance. Besides, she had spit in his face. She had earned her pain.

The riding crop was next. The girls all flinched at each "crack" that resounded as their mother's flesh was struck. No part of her body was left unharmed. She moaned exquisitely as the guard struck her gaping slit repeatedly. Her eyes were pleading now, her body covered with sweat and bruises. She seemed to be begging the Prince for mercy, but her voice was stilled by her gag and all that could emerge were her violent whines and moans.

While the guard was mercilessly applying the crop to the woman's body, the Prince was amusing himself with the helpless and exposed bodies of her daughters. He delicately caressed their small, firm tits, squeezing here, pinching there. The girls all tried to shy away from him as he stroked their bodies, but the chains held them pinioned. Finally, he signaled to the guard to stop. He approached Madam Paralova. She was hanging dejectedly, moaning.

"Ah, Madam Paralova, have you had enough?" he asked her. Forlornly, she nodded yes, hopeful to stop her abuse. But it was not yet time. "No, I think not," the Prince said, answering his own question. "One more treat and then I'll give you the opportunity to beg."

Madam Paralova's eyes pleaded desperately. She had been brave, even noble, in her refusal to surrender her and her daughters' virtue. But that time had passed. She would be ashamed and sorrowful later for her surrender, but now, all she wanted was a surcease of pain.

A servant handed the Prince the electric wand. Madam Paralova's eyes widened with terror. She did not know what the Prince held in his hand, but she knew that it would be the instrument of her further torment. She knew that the Prince would save the worst for last. The Prince rubbed the wand over her body, poking and prodding her. She was trembling now, futilely attempting to communicate her earnest desire to serve the Prince in any way that he chose. The Prince could hear the whining and pleading of the girls behind his back as they desperately tried to obtain mercy for their mother. The Prince ordered the woman's gag removed.

"Please, oh, please," she cried, "no more, please! I'll do what you want, please no more!"

The Prince smiled as he applied the wand to her left nipple. "Crack!' The electric charge tore into her breast. She stiffened and cried out in agony. "Crack!" Her right breast absorbed another jolt.

"I beg you to stop!" she screamed, "I beg you!" The Prince circled her and applied the wand to her rear opening. "Crack!" She was blubbering now, having lost all control. There was one more obvious target for the Prince's cruelty. He stood before her and pushed the wand up deep into her pleasure gorge. This time the "crack" of the electric charge was muffled as it was absorbed by the interior of the poor woman's sex. She howled with pain.

Now she was ready. The Prince let her regain her senses. When she was recovered enough, he addressed her.

"Have you had enough, Madam Paralova?"

"Oh, yes, please, please," she murmured.

"I want you to beg me to fuck you up the ass, Madam Paralova," the Prince told her. "And then you will beg me to let you lick you daughter's cunts."

The woman lifted her head weakly. Her eyes were red, her makeup streaked across her face, her hair wildly tangled. Her lips trembled, her face contorted as she spoke. Her voice was low, almost imperceptible.

"I beg you," she said.

"No, Madam Paralova," the Prince replied in a stern, unyielding voice. "You must say it all."

A loud sob escaped the woman's lips. She raised her voice, anxious that she be heard, praying that she had to say it only once. "I beg you to fuck my ass. I beg you to let me lick my daughter's cunts." She sobbed in defeat.

"Why, gladly, Madam Paralova," the Prince taunted her, "you had only to ask."

He signaled the woman to be released. She could not stand and had to be supported by the arms of the guards. She was dragged over to one of the large pillows on the floor and draped over it. A servant hurried over to her and applied a dollop of lubricant to her ass for the ease of the Prince's prick. He had it out and was stroking it. He walked over to the dangling sisters. Their eyes were pinned to the hard, red, cock.

"Who shall be first, my dears?" the Prince asked. They were in no shape to answer. The nightmarish series of events that had witnessed had rendered them mute. Even if they had not been gagged, they would have been unable to reply.

"I think youngest first," the Prince said, approaching Katya. Her arms were lowered and released. Two guards took her in hand and pushed her to her knees in front of her moaning mother. Madam Paralova looked up and spoke softly to her, tears flowing down her face. Katya was crying too, but her mother's words seemed to calm her. She nodded complaisantly. As the Prince prepared to mount her mother, the guards leaned her back, spreading her legs. She closed her eyes.

"Now Madam Paralova," the Prince addressed the abject woman, "you don't have to make her come, just get her good and wet."

There was no need to bind the mother's arms. She had no more resistance in her. She cried out as the Prince pressed his cock in her small rectal hole, tearing her flesh.

"Ahhhhhh," the Prince moaned. "You have a wonderfully tight ass, Madam Paralova. Now start licking."

The woman lowered her head between her youngest daughter's thighs and tenderly tongued the virgin gash between them. Katya placed her still bound hands over her face in shame and cried. The Prince was a patient man and slowly stroked his cock back and forth in Madam Paralova's bowels while the woman sucked and licked at her daughter's crevasse. Katya stiffened when she first felt the hot tongue glide along the lips of her sex. Gradually, however, she began to soften as the strokes of her mother's tongue drove her to unavoidable pleasure. When the Prince was satisfied that she had begun to respond passionately to her mother's efforts, he called out for Nadine. As Nadine was forced to spread her legs and offer her pussy to her mother's lips, Katya was dragged away. When he saw Nadine's eyes begin to flutter, her thighs begin to jerk excitedly, he called for Nadia.

Nadia abjectly spread her thighs, but soon was moaning and squirming under her mother's desperate efforts. The Prince was stroking Madam Paralova's ass now in earnest as he allowed his lust to take command. Both Nadia and her mother were moaning now. The Prince reached below the mother's stomach and began to stroke her moistened pussy. She responded immediately, pressing her slit against his hand, energizing her oral abuse of Nadia's sex. Nadia responded in turn by moaning loudly and bucking her hips.

The Prince waited until Nadia was in the throws of her orgasm to spill his seed deep into Madam Paralova's bowels. Feeling the hot release of the Prince's spunk, she, in turn, achieved release, squeezing her thighs and pressing up to gather in the Prince's throbbing cock.

It had been a memorable spectacle. As he rose from between the mother's legs, the Prince observed that Katya and Nadine had already been collared and gagged. Their slave bracelets were being added to their ankles and wrists. When Nadia and Mrs. Paralova had been similarly accoutered, he ordered them to be delivered to his suite.

That night he fucked the mother roundly in his bedroom suite while the girls, their hands tied to chains from the ceiling, watched, naked, from the foot of his bed. Since then he had still not fucked them, although he had entertained himself with their bodies. Nadia and Nadine had become practiced cunnaliguists, while little Katya had been schooled in the art of sucking a prick. And the mother, well, once the reserve of civilization had been torn away from her, she had become like a bitch in heat. He had to admit that there was something to fucking an older woman. Her body was fuller and more mature, softer in places where the young beauties he was used to using were hard. She never said a word when they fucked, never again uttered a word of protest at his abuse of her daughters.

But now that the ship was approaching the dock in the Calipha Harbor, the time had drawn near for decisions. A decision about Sergi's request, a decision about what to do about the delightful Paralova females and time for a decision about this so called Paul Turner. It was also time for him to sample this Carmella himself.

CHAPTER THIRTEEN

Aboud sat across the room from Jennine. They were in her sitting room, ensconced in large comfortable easy chairs. Jennine was sipping a spry, light chardonnay, Aboud nothing. He was not in the mood for relaxed and clever repartee. He was on a mission.

"You know, Jennine, that I have served the Prince loyally for many years. I have never asked for anything, no special treatment, no rewards."

"Yes, yes, Aboud, I know all of this." Jennine replied.

"I have the right to select a personal body slave, something I have never done."

"You have that right Aboud, but not Carmella."

"Why not Carmella?" Aboud's face was set with determination. He had lasted as long as he could. He burned with desire for Carmella, yearned for her, yearned to possess her. In the many weeks since she had been sent "upstairs" he had sublimated his passion on the bodies of the slaves within his reach. He had tormented them unmercifully, far beyond what was necessary for their training. Twice he had been "reminded" of the need for circumspection in the handling of new slaves. And now he had been called upstairs to speak to Jennine, two steps away from the Prince himself.

"Listen, Aboud," Jennine said determinedly, "there must be fifty well trained slaves here available for your use, many of them as pretty, or prettier than Carmella. The upstairs girls are not available as body slaves to trainers. You know that. The reputation of this House is made by the especially well trained, responsive and alluring females who are selected for this floor. They are one in a hundred. Carmella is just that, one in a hundred. The answer is just plain no."

"You could intercede for me with the Prince," Aboud pointed out. "I have trained well over a hundred slaves for him. Half the women on this floor have passed through my hands. I'll promise him to do even better, I swear it. I must have Carmella. It is driving me mad!"

"I am sorry for you, Aboud," Jennine replied, pausing to take a sip of her wine. "But it is just impossible. Carmella is the Prince's property. He can do with her as he wishes."

"But that's my point…" Aboud interrupted.

"I'm telling you that it's impossible!" Jennine's voice was raised now, imperative."

"And why is it impossible?" Aboud demanded.

"Because she's been sold. That's why!"

"Sold?" Aboud was stunned. Had he acted too late? "Sold to whom?"

"That's none of your concern," Jennine replied.

Aboud jumped from his chair. "I'm making it my concern!" he yelled. "I want to know who!"

Jennine was taken aback by Aboud's vehemence. His entire body was taut with anger. His hands were clenched, his face red. She did not want to tell him who had purchased Carmella, but she knew that if she did not tell him, he was capable of beating it out of her.

"To Sergi Krasjnavic," she said softly.

"Sergi Krasjnavic? He's an animal. You can't do that!"

"Aboud, I'm not doing anything. I'm obeying orders. Besides, what difference does it make? Sure, she could last here for maybe two or three years. But then she'd be sold off to who knows who. In ten years she would be useless as a whore. Probably less."

"But Krasjnavic is a vicious animal. She'll be dead in a month."

"A month, a year, ten years, what does it matter?" Jennine was standing now, her blood was up. "You know as well as I do that these females are beasts of burden. They became animals the moment they were 'kissed on the hand'. What happens to them is of no consequence. How many of those hundred or so women you so skillfully acclimated to their chains are here today? Twenty? And where are all the rest? Do you care? Of course not. Carmella is no different. She is a pleasing animal, no more human than a dog or a cat. And like a dog or a cat, once she stops being pleasing she will cease to exist."

Aboud was crushed. He sat back down in his chair, his hands on his head.

Jennine continued, "In fact we are moving on two slaves today. Carmella is just one of them. I need to make room for the new ones, the fresh ones. It happens all the time."

"But Carmella is still fresh, she's new. It's been only a few months," Aboud said, plaintively.

"I'm telling you Aboud, it's out of my hands. Forget her."

He knew that he had shot his bolt. She was right. It was out of her hands. There was only one person who could countermand an order from the Prince. The Prince. He would have to go see him. Today.

* * * * * *

Carmella was lying in her bed, overjoyed. Next to her was the pretty, little Danish girl, Veronica, who she had fallen in love with. It was late to be allowed to stay in bed. By this time, on most days, she would be attending lunch in the bar, or locked in a bedroom awaiting her guest. But

Carmella was determined to make the most of it. Although her hands were affixed to the front of her collar, which in turn was affixed to a chain from the headboard, Carmella was free to gaze longingly in Veronica's star like, blue eyes. She had been surprised when her room assignment had been changed yesterday, at least a week ahead of schedule. But she enthralled to learn that Veronica would be her partner.

Their hands were intertwined. They had just finished lovemaking, passionate kissing and rubbing their bodies together. Carmella had placed her right leg between Veronica's and pressed her lusting pussy up against hers. Slowly, the two women rubbed their slits together, gyrating their hips, entwining their tongues. Carmella longed to stroke Veronica's sex, with its prominent labial lips, and the large hard kernel at the top. Veronica was well blessed with a larger than average, and very sensitive, clitoris. When they had been able, on those rare free days they had together, Carmella loved to flick it gently with her fingers as she delved her tongue inside.

After languorous minutes, Carmella whispered to Veronica, "Let me suck your pussy."

Veronica smiled and replied in delicately accented English, "Oh yes, Carmella, please."

Veronica was able to kneel close to the headboard, facing it, and spread her legs wide. There was just enough room on the chain for Carmella to sneak inside, and raise her lips to the beautiful, hairless sex. She licked Veronica's labial divide down its length, bringing a moan of pleasure to the diminutive girl. Her blond hair, longer than Carmella's, had grown long enough to fall down her face as she leaned over an accepted the torrid caresses from her lover.

Her pussy was burning with lust, and Veronica slid down slightly to let Carmella have access to her bud of pleasure. Carmella sucked on it gently, playing with it with her tongue. Veronica was more vocal now as she approached her climax. She spread her legs wider, pressing her now gushing crevasse onto Carmella's face. "Ahhhhhhhhhhhhh!" she moaned loudly as she felt the first spasms of delight. "Oh! Oh! Oh!" she called out as her orgasm overwhelmed her.

When her orgasm had faded, Veronica slid down and kissed Carmella on the mouth. "And now you," she said. "I want to lick you."

Carmella obliged the panting, sweating woman. When she was perched on Veronica's mouth, Carmella began to sigh and moan as the woman's expert tongue and lips drove her to pleasure. Twice she came, the second time more intensely than the first. Finally, she was spent and she slid her body back down the bed, rubbing it up against Veronica's, seeking her heat.

Now they were floating in the tender afterworld brought on by loving sex. Carmella kissed Veronica's lips and whispered to her, "I love you, Veronica."

Veronica had just opened her mouth to answer when the door burst open. The women looked up in surprise. Entering the room were not the small, brown skinned servants whose duty it was to waken and unlock the girls in time for their duties. Instead, it was two tall black guards, intent expressions on their faces. They had leather hoods and bindings in their hands.

It was always disconcerting to the other girls when an "upstairs girl" was sold on. For that reason, Jennine usually arranged for the women to be removed from the floor as discretely as possible. With the varying schedules, it sometimes took days for a girl to be missed. And by then a new girl had taken her place. Carmella and Veronica had been isolated for just this reason. The joyful interlude that they had experienced had been due to the fact that their removal would be done when the other girls were off of the floor.

"Good morning slaves," the larger of the two guards said in a lilting, melodious accent, the voice of the African savannah. "You are going on a little trip today. We've come to get you ready."

The two women knew at once what was meant by a little trip. Of course they knew that their time as exemplars of the pinnacle of female pulchritude would not last forever. But when the downfall came, it was always a surprise.

Exceeding all the bounds of what was permitted, the women began to protest and cry out. Carmella turned to Veronica and clutched her hands, calling out, "No! No! No!" Veronica screamed and struggled as her collar was unfastened from the headboard and she was dragged out of the bed.

It was an easy task for the two men to pull Veronica to her feet. While one of them encircled her with his arms, the other began to pull a hood over Veronica's head. The hood was a standard traveling hood and came with a large wedge of leather that served as a built in gag. Carmella's last sight of Veronica's face was the hood descending over her head and the gag being forced between her teeth.

Carmella was crying, sobbing uncontrollably. The men ignored her as they freed Veronica's hands from her collar and brought them around her back. Once they were joined there, the smaller guard produced a small belt that he used to circle Veronica's upper arms, pulling them together tightly. Veronica moaned as her arms were forcibly pulled taut behind her back. Her breasts jutted out, now in a proper state for presentation to her new owner.

The women's ownership never really passed from the Caliphate. It was more of a lease really, a bond posted for their return, a monthly rental calculated, payment in advance made for the entire lease term. And if the girl did not return, well, the bond was considered payment enough. Her fate was of really no consequence.

Veronica was now hooded and gagged, bound helplessly. The guards affixed a short chain between her ankles. They were entrusted with the Prince's property until the goods were actually delivered into the hands of her new owner. A panicked slave might attempt to run away, foolishly, of course, since she could not see. But she might damage herself in the process and so no chances were to be taken.

The men pushed Veronica to her knees and fastened her collar to one of the posts of the bed. She was going nowhere. They then turned their attention to Carmella.

"Now, pretty one," the larger, meaner looking one spoke, "it's your turn. But first I want to fuck that pretty little pussy of yours." His voice was harsh, made strange by the almost musical accent.

"I've been watching you and I've been waiting for my chance to put my prick in you." The fearsome black giant began to disrobe. Carmella revolted against the promised assault. Once again, a new torment confronted her. What had she done? How had she sinned? What new terror awaited her?

As the man crept onto the bed, Carmella kicked out at him. He grabbed her foot and before she new it, the grinning black man had insinuated himself between her legs. Vainly, she tried to press her thighs together as she cried out at this new insult. "Oh god, Veronica! Veronica!" she called out.

The man's strong thighs pushed Carmella's apart. She felt the head of his prick press against the entrance of her still wet crevasse. She bucked and heaved in a fruitless attempt to throw the man off of her. His prick pressed on relentlessly, passing her soft, tender lips, entering her, piercing her.

As the cock slid home, Carmella emitted a doleful cry. She had serviced many a cock since she had been enslaved, of all colors, shapes and sizes. Black men, African and American had fucked her, oriental, Caucasian, Hispanic, Arabic and even a Jew, had possessed her. She had dutifully, and even enthusiastically, served them all. None had been as insulting and as dehumanizing as the cock that now violated her body.

The man pressed his weight down upon Carmella, his mass crushing her bound hands against her chest. She felt a hand grab her hair, pulling her head back, and another press against her cheeks. Her mouth was forced open and she felt the man's tongue fill her oral cavity. She knew she should cease her struggles. She knew that she was powerless to prevent this demeaning rape. But her whole being was filled with revulsion as the powerful man plunged in and out of her defenseless canal, insulted her mouth.

With a groan of pleasure, the man jetted his cum inside of her. She felt him tense as he pounded his hips against hers. He finally slowed, his muscles loosened, and he was done.

The other guard turned her onto her stomach. He pulled her hips up and back and pressed his iron hard flesh into her anal opening. Carmella was defeated now and, ironically, her surrender to her fate made the entrance of the thick, hot meat, easy. She was too filled with despair to cry any more. She let the man have his way, grunting and groaning as he enjoyed the heat of her bowels. She felt his spunk shoot inside her and was grateful when he softened and slipped out of her rear.

The men quickly released her collar from the headboard and yanked Carmella to her feet. She did not resist as the hood was pulled over her head and the thick, invasive gag pushed into her mouth. Her hands were locked behind her, her arms forced together. She felt the chain affixed to her ankles. She was deprived of sight and speech, she was headed towards an unknown fate. Passively, she let herself be pulled from the room.

The progress was slow as the chains between the two women's feet forced them to take tiny steps. The guards were patient, guiding them through the empty corridors. Carmella heard a door open and felt soft fabric beneath her feet. She heard a woman's voice, laughing, a familiar voice, Jennine's.

"Ah, Mr. Kubyashi, your slave has arrived," Jennine said. The guards halted Carmella's progress. She guessed that they were in Jennine's sitting room. She remembered her joy at finding Jennine here. Her heart sunk as she realized that she was facing yet another betrayal.

She heard a man's voice, a familiar voice. She had not heard the name before, but she knew the voice. He had used her, more than once. He was a slender but well muscled man. Japanese. At first he had been deferential, polite, as he requested her to open herself, to caress her own flesh in front of him. He had then locked her hands behind her back and the torment had begun.

It seemed that Mr. Kubyashi was an expert on human anatomy. He began by pressing against certain pressure points in Carmella's arms and legs. The pain had been piercing, immediate. Soon she was pleading for him to stop as he sought out and found the precise locations of tender nerve endings all around her body and manipulated them until impulses of pain shot to her brain. Each session had lasted more than two hours. He had entered her with his long, hard cock and held her still as he coaxed out her loud and frantic exclamations of pain. When he came, he used his hands to heighten her torment and his pulses of pleasure were accompanied by Carmella's screams.

Carmella's knees weakened as she contemplated being turned over to his control. "Not me," she said to herself, desperately, "Please God, not me!"

But it was Veronica, her lover, that Mr. Kubyashi had come to claim.

"Miss Jennine," Kubyashi spoke in almost perfect English, "thank you for you courtesies. I am sure that Veronica will bring me much pleasure."

Carmella heard Veronica moan. She too recognized the voice, as Kubyashi's unique and terrible form of torment had been well known across the second floor. Carmella shamefully regretted her earlier prayer, as she knew the cruel fate that was in store for her beautiful, tender lover. Carmella tried to pull away from the strong hand that held her arm. She wanted to plead with Jennine, beg her to spare Veronica this fate. Her efforts were futile. She heard Veronica's muffled cry as Kubyashi apparently took possession of his new slave.

"Please don't forget us Mr. Kubyashi," Jennine said. "I have several new girls who will delight you."

"I will certainly return, Ms. Jennine," Kubyashi replied. "Your females are most exquisite."

"From you, that is a great compliment, Mr. Kubyashi," Jennine replied.

Carmella heard Veronica being escorted from the room. She was doubly crushed at her lover's fate and the shattering abandonment she felt as Jennine revealed her cruel, callous nature. Carmella had caressed her often, lovingly, thankful for her softness and warmth. She despised herself for her stupidity.

Her stomach knotted as she heard the door close. She started to tremble as she awaited whatever cruel fate was in store for her. She felt the heat of a body approach hers. A soft, feminine hand grabbed her breast. Another seized her sex. She heard Jennine's heartless voice.

"Oh, Carmella, I will miss you. You are a fine whore."

Carmella began to cry beneath her hood. She tried to escape from what were now revolting caresses. The guards were holding her arms and so her efforts accomplished no more than shaking of her torso. She felt Jennine's fingers enter her pussy and then grab her tender nub. She had it between her fingers and her thumb and pressed hard. A shooting pain paralyzed Carmella. She stiffened and moaned in agony. Jennine pressed all the harder. Carmella tried to double over, to move her pelvis away from Jennine's tormenting hand. But she was held fast

After she was satisfied that Carmella was under control, Jennine dismissed the guards. "I can handle this slave. You may go until I call you."

The guards dutifully released Carmella and left the room. The excruciating pressure on Carmella's clit had eased, but Jennine still held it firmly between her fingers and thumb. "Control yourself, Carmella," the stern woman said. "We have a little time to spend together before you go and I would enjoy an excuse to put a lash to your flesh one more time. And your new master would be upset at you being all marked up because of disobedience. It would be a very poor start."

Being thoroughly gagged, Carmella had no answer for Jennine's taunts. She determined to get a hold on herself, not to give this bitch the satisfaction of seeing her cringe and cry. The river had taken another turn, that's all. She had survived so far and she would continue to survive at all costs.

Jennine placed her lips on Carmella's breast. She sucked it fiercely, pulling at with her lips. Her hand worked deeper into Carmella's pussy, working it open, bringing on the lubrication that signaled arousal. She moved to the other breast, giving it the same rough attention. "You are truly a delightful creature Carmella," she said softly as she raised her head. "It's a pity you have been sold. I was looking forward to many nights with your lips between my legs. I would remove your gag and have you suck at my clit, but you would probably plead and beg not to be sent away. It would be so boring, a trite ending to pleasurable memories."

Jennine grabbed Carmella's nubbin once again and pulled her across the room. Carmella could take only baby steps due to the chains that bound her ankles. But the pressure on her little bud was painful and she shuffled her feet quickly to keep up. She felt herself turned around and then pulled back. She ended by sitting on Jennine's lap.

Jennine pushed Carmella's knees apart and again took possession of her pleasure mound. Her other arm circled around Carmella and grabbed her left breast, squeezing it harshly. "I'm going to make you come, Carmella, just to prove to you once and for all what a whore you really are." Carmella tried to press her knees back together to deny Jennine access to her pussy. But Jennine had a firm grasp on her pussy and began to squeeze the aching, abused clit again. Carmella moaned in pain and spread her thighs. The chain on her ankles was just long enough to allow Carmella to widen the space between her knees.

"That's it Carmella. That's a good little whore. Now lean back and enjoy it while I tell you about your new master."

She could feel the stiff nipples of Jennine's breasts in her back. Her lips were on her throat, kissing and sucking on her flesh. Carmella vainly fought against the tide of passion that was arising in her. Since her mouth was sealed, she could only breathe through her nose, and her efforts to suck in air caused her chest to rise and fall rapidly. Jennine was an expert with a pussy and toyed with Carmella, bringing her close to orgasm and then retreating. Carmella could not help herself, she moaned with pleasure, spreading her knees open as wide as she could, crossing her ankles to permit maximum access to her burning sex. Being blinded by the hood, deprived of sight, made Carmella's helplessness more intense. "They have taken everything from me," she thought. "Everything."

"Let yourself go, Carmella, moan and groan for me. Be a good pet. For that's what you are, you know, a pleasure giving pet," Jennine told the desolate woman as she stroked and massaged her soft, soaking quim. "You don't still think of yourself as a human being do you? Human beings have pride and dignity, and you have neither. Just look at yourself, your pussy creams at the slightest touch. You are a reactive animal who we have taught little tricks."

Carmella tried to deny the cruel words of her mistress. But she could not. She was a reactive creature, coming almost on command, kneeling like a puppy, lapping at anonymous pricks and cunts, degrading herself daily.

Her fever was rising higher. She knew that soon she would be unable to prevent the waves of pleasure to overwhelm her. As she was inexorably building to her climax, driven by the relentless stroking of her sex, she heard, through her passionate fog, Jennine whisper in her leather covered ear.

"Your new master, Carmella, you know him well" she said. "He has a little trick he likes to use to heighten his enjoyment while he whips the tits of young females. You know Carmella, the little thing with the sandpaper."

Jennine had timed her shocking disclosure perfectly. Carmella was over the top. She rocked and moaned through her gag as her crevasse pulsed around the fingers inside her. She felt Jennine bite down on her neck harshly and squeeze her right breast. Had she not been gagged, her voice would have filled the room.

As her passion cooled, Carmella took in what Jennine had told her. Sergi, her new master! A stab of cold ran through her heart, her stomach quailed. "Oh god, no, please, don't let it be true!" she thought. Her moans of pleasure turned in an instant into cries of woe. She had spent four days under his sadistic torments. To be owned by him! Carmella had no doubt that her life would be a stream of the most excruciating tortures. Already, she could feel the fear chilling her to the very bone.

Jennine observed Carmella's obvious distress at her news. She wished that she could be there when Sergi took possession of her. It would be amusing.

"Thank you for this pleasant interlude, Carmella," Jennine said sarcastically as she pushed the miserable young woman off of her lap. Carmella sank to her knees. Her body was quaking with her sobs, all but smothered by her gag.

Walking across the room, Jennine pulled a cord by the window. The cord rang a bell in the anteroom to her chambers. The two guards came in.

"You may take her," Jennine said coldly while she eyed the forlorn figure kneeling before her. "Goodbye

Carmella," she said. "I doubt that we'll see you again. Sergi does go through girls so quickly. I'll have such pleasurable memories of you though. Oh, and by the way, you'll have a few days to fret about your miserable fate. The Prince has heard what a wonderful slut you are. He wants to fuck you and have you suck his cock before he delivers you to your new master. Who knows, if you do a god job, maybe he'll change his mind? But I doubt it. He has so many skilled and beautiful whores to choose from." She turned to the guards. "Take her away."

CHAPTER FOURTEEN

Aboud drove like a madman to get to the Prince's mansion. It was a little over sixty miles from the House of Adeem. Pushing 100 miles an hour, Aboud calculated that he would get their in about 40 minutes. Not knowing that Carmella would be following along the same road in a little while, albeit at a more leisurely pace, Aboud believed that every second counted. "I must get there before Carmella is delivered to that beast!" Aboud thought frantically.

He had tried to telephone, but he got no further than the secretary to the Prince's major domo, Rashid. "Yes," he had been told, she would take a message. Yes, she understood it was urgent. Was there a telephone number he could be reached at?

Aboud knew that the voice on the other end of the line was a naked and collared slave. She would no more disturb Rashid than she would refuse an order from a master. He knew that his only chance was to get there, somehow gain access to Rashid and, through him, to the Prince. It was almost hopeless, but he was determined to try.

After what seemed an eternity, Aboud screeched the dust covered four by four to a halt in front of the main entrance to the Prince's mansion. He had been there only once, to deliver some newly trained slaves for the Prince's pleasure, and had come in through the cellar entrance in the back. He had not gone further than the anteroom to the Prince's private dungeon. He knew he had to go in the front or he would be barred from going any further this time as well.

He ran up the steps and pushed open the large mahogany door. Three of the Sudanese guards were lurking at the entrance, almost certainly armed. A clerk sat at a desk about ten feet from the door.

"What's your business?" he asked disdainfully. Aboud was not outfitted in the raiment of a social guest. He was wearing his working clothes, a grey tee shirt and shorts. He did not have time to change. He knew that he would have to bluff his way through.

"I have an appointment to see Rashid," he announced, disguising his breathlessness. "I need to see him immediately!"

"Well, you're not in the book," the clerk, a mousy, pinched faced bureaucrat, replied. "I'll call and see if you're expected."

Leisurely, the clerk dialed an extension. Aboud could hear a woman's voice answer. "How may I serve you, Master?" the obsequious voice asked.

"Is Master Rashid expecting a visitor? A Mister ...," he looked up at Aboud quizzically.

"Aboud," he was answered. "I am a trainer at the House of Adeem.

"...a Mister Aboud," the clerk uttered into the phone. "No appointments at all? Okay." He hung up the phone.

Aboud was desperate. "I must get in to speak to Rashid!" he yelled. The guards shifted their bodies, now interested at the developments at the doorway.

"Don't yell at me," the clerk responded snottily. "No appointment, no admittance."

"But I must get through!" Aboud yelled. He tried to dash past the desk. One of the hulking Sudanese guards stood in his way. He was about the same size and build as Aboud. But he had two other guards to help him.

Blinded by his need, Aboud pushed at the guard. After that he remembered only a crushing blow to his head. One of the guards had brought the handle of his pistol down on Aboud's cranium. He went out like a light.

The clerk had risen from his chair. He was puny next to the mountainous Sudanese. But he had authority.

"Take him down to the cellars and throw him in a cell. I'll report this matter to Rashid."

* * * * * *

Shortly after Aboud was dragged, limp and unconscious, to a cell, Carmella was being led down a set of stairs in the rear of the House of Adeem. It would not do for her to be seen by the other girls and the less the guests knew about the inner workings of the House, the better.

She was led to a small white van, perhaps the very one she had been brought in. She was pushed inside, onto her stomach, down to the roughly carpeted floor. Her ankle chain was loosened only to have one end looped over her bound hands. It was pulled tight and first one leg, and then the other, was raised up until her ankles touched her wrists. The chain was fastened off and she was left there, hog tied, and ready for her journey.

There was no need for subtlety or subterfuge in the transport of slaves in Calipha. It was all perfectly legal. Any official notice of Carmella's transport would see it as routine, although a curious security officer might take the time to flip Carmella over, to admire her belly and breasts. It was not unknown for a slave transport to be waylaid temporarily, to the profit of its driver, while the officer, or officers, tried out one of the Caliphate's beauteous sluts.

But there would be no interruptions to Carmella's trip. The van proceeded lazily over the desert highway, rocking Carmella gently. She had turned herself onto her side, the better to ease the strain on her shoulders, the rough contact between her nipples and the coarse rug. She tried to drive all thoughts from her mind, letting the gentle rhythm of the ride lull her into a dreamlike state. But each time that she dozed off, a bump in the road, the swerve of the van to avoid the ubiquitous desert life, brought her to consciousness. She remembered the last time she had been in a van. She was not the same person as that terrified, young girl. That girl was blissfully unaware of the torments that awaited her. Carmella now knew only too well what the future portended.

She cried softly, thinking of Jeb and Aboud. What she would give to be able to spend even a few moments in their arms, in the arms of someone who cared for her and about what happened to her. Even though she had not seen Aboud since she had been 'promoted' from the training areas, she remembered their last night together. She had sensed that he had some feeling for her, a feeling he could only express with the kindness and pleasure of his caresses. But Carmella was ignorant of the efforts of Jeb and Aboud to save her. She had no inkling that she was being transported to a place where she would be literally within fifty yards of both of them.

The van pulled into the compound that contained the Prince's mansion and drove to the rear. Carmella heard the driver's door slam and the sound of feet on gravel as he walked to the building to check in. A few moments later, two servants emerged with him. She heard the door to the rear of the van slide open and felt hands on her ankles. Once they were freed, she was dragged out and frog marched inside.

A supervisor met them. Carmella could not understand what they said since, having no need to deal with guests and no present need to communicate with Carmella, the men spoke Arabic.

"Take this slut upstairs, they're waiting for her," the supervisor told the two black haired, white-coated servants. Carmella was taken up a small elevator to the second floor of the mansion. She was led down the hall to the east wing, where the pleasure slaves were housed. A burly matron took custody of her from the servants and led her into the dormitory and over to a large, white tiled bathroom. Two slaves were waiting, naked and collared.

Carmella's hood was removed. The mid afternoon light blinded her momentarily. Her mouth was cramped from the gag and she stretched her jaw in relief. She did not see the matron, but observed the two pretty, young slaves standing in front of her. She started to speak to them, "Where…."

A resounding "crack" echoed in the room as the matron administered a sturdy slap across Carmella's face. "Silence!" she commanded. "You're not an upstairs girl now, whore! The Prince wants to see you and stuff his cock up your ass. But he wants you to be pretty. These slaves will bathe you and decorate your body. If I hear any talking, I'll give you ten strokes with the cane across your cunt. Do you understand?"

Suddenly, the daily terror of the training rooms was brought back to Carmella. She had almost forgotten, having spent the last three months in the comparatively liberated confines of the second floor of the House of Adeem. She fought back tears as she respectfully answered the matron, "Yes, madam."

She was washed quickly; her eyes were made up, her breasts and lower lips rouged. She was given an enema, so that the Prince's cock would not be befouled by her bodily wastes.

When they were done, the women all sank silently to their knees and waited.

After a short while, the matron returned. She was holding a thick leather collar and matching bracelets. She removed the smooth leather bonds that Carmella had been granted upon her ascension to the second floor and replaced them with these coarse, rough ones. She was just a slave, like all the rest, thought Carmella as the collar clicked shut around her neck. Her hands were bound behind her back and a soft, black blindfold was wrapped around her head, blocking out all light. A long, penis shaped gag was thrust in her mouth.

The matron paused to appreciate the fine form of this demoted whore. When the Prince was done with her tonight, she would have her lap at her cunt.

A slight chain was affixed to the ring in the front of Carmella's collar and she felt herself tugged forwards. Blindly, she was led along one corridor after another. The Prince had a massive suite in the west wing and that was Carmella's destination. She could not appreciate the fine appointments of the Prince's sitting room, elegant regency style sofas and chairs covered with soft yellow cloth, golden threaded curtains surrounding large, arching windows. The rug was soft and thick, the sideboards and coffee tables made of dark, finely polished oak.

Carmella was led to the center of the room. A chain was lowered from the ceiling and locked to her bracelets behind her back. It was pulled up just enough to ensure that Carmella stood erect, at her full height. She heard soft footsteps retreating through the room and the opening and closing of a heavy door. And there she awaited her presentation to the Prince, for the time being, at least, her master.

*   *   *   *   *   *   *

In a room on the third floor of the mansion, located a stone's throw from the room directly above the Prince's sitting room, Jeb sat brooding. He had had no luck in his search for Carmella. As far as he had been able to learn, there were five major whorehouses in Calipha and about ten smaller ones. All of them were staffed with slaves. And, he found out, slaves were often sold out of the country completely. Not sold, really, leased.

Every slave who served in Calipha had been judicially enslaved by fiat of the Royal Court. The fact that they were serving legitimate, although certainly tainted, sentences for violations of Calipha criminal statutes, meant that they were technically not slaves, but prisoners, criminals. It was a simple matter of a contract between the government of Calipha, embodied by the Prince, and any individual or entity worldwide, and the 'prisoners' could be shipped off as indentured labor. They were simply serving their sentences abroad.

This made the enslavement of the women technically legal. Not that it would stand up in any Western country. But in literally hundreds of sovereign states around the globe, where the rule of law was thin, it was good enough.

So Carmella could be anywhere, in Calipha, in Thailand, Kazakhstan, Chad, Indonesia, Benin, Laos, even China or in South America, in any place where the writ of the government did not run. Calipha exported several hundred slaves a year. What chance did he have of ever finding Carmella?

Out of the corner of his eye, Jeb noted his 'assistant', Amy, cleaning up some papers he had left spread across his desk. She was naked, as she had remained since being enslaved, and her breasts jiggled invitingly as she moved back and forth with his files. As she passed Jeb's chair, she stumbled and knocked against the side table where Jeb had set his afternoon glass of wine. The glass tottered and then fell. The dark red wine cascaded from the glass onto the rug.

"I'm sorry, Mr. Turner. I'll clean it up."

Jeb felt rage rise in his breast. "Why don't you watch where your going, you stupid cunt!" he spit at the girl.

Amy turned, startled at the unusual outburst from her 'employer'. For aside from sucking his cock and being subject to his other sexual needs, their relationship had been largely cordial, like any other administrative assistant and her boss. He had even had her sleeping quarters moved from the dungeon to his suite. This spared her the random rapes and beatings that other serving slaves were subject to. Momentarily forgetting her station, Amy replied in an annoyed tone, "I told you that I would clean it up!"

That was all that Jeb needed. His eyes clouded over, his hands clenched. "What did you say, slave?" he spat at her.

"I, I'm sorry, Mr. Turner, it won't happen again," Amy pleaded. She realized that she had gone too far.

Jeb leapt from his chair and slapped Amy across the face. She fell over, unbalanced by this unexpected blow. Jeb had never struck her, had never struck any of the slaves. He had often watched with mesmerized fascination as they had been whipped or beaten. He had never even reported any dissatisfaction with a slave so that she would be punished. He had drawn the line at that. But now, all of the frustration that he felt at his failure to locate Carmella boiled over, and the focus of his ire was Amy.

"Get up, you fucking worthless cunt!" he yelled.

Amy meekly rose to her feet, cowering. Jeb grabbed her wrist and dragged her to the column set in the far side of the room. It had sat there unused and barely noticed during Jeb's occupancy of the suite, but now he was determined to put it to use. He quickly fastened first one, then the other, of Amy's wrists to the chain that hung down from the ceiling. He pulled it taut so that Amy was standing on her toes, her body fully extended.

"Oh, master, please, I'm sorry, please, please!" She had reverted to the rules of her enslavement, realizing that some line had been crossed and that her right to call Jeb 'Mr. Turner' had been abjured.

Jeb slapped her across the face. "Shut up!" he yelled. He looked around and saw a cloth napkin from his lunch still sitting on the dining table. He walked over and grabbed it. Returning to Amy, he gathered it in a ball and stuffed it in her mouth.

Amy was terrified. Jeb's suite had been a haven for her. She had spent her time in the dungeon, had been beaten and whipped repeatedly there. Since coming to work for Jeb, she had only been raped once or twice, if you didn't count the many times Jeb had fucked her. She had often talked in little whispers with the slave girls who were stationed in Jeb's suite about what slavery was like and she had heard terrifying stories. Now, she was petrified that she would be sent away.

Jeb's thoughts had not gone that far. He wanted someone to suffer for his pain, his guilt. Right now, Amy fit the bill.

He walked over to the cabinet that he knew contained implements of abuse. Rashid had shown it to him when he was given the suite, but he hadn't looked in it since. He selected a short, single tasseled whip with a knotted end.

He walked directly over to where Amy hung by her writs and, without pause, lit into her.

"Whack!" "Crack!" "Whack!" He hit her three times across the back. Amy screamed in pain and tried to dance away from the whip. But there was not much lead on the chain that held her and Jeb was able to reach her easily.

"Crack!" "Crack!" "Crack!" The leather thong found Amy's flesh again, this time across her legs and thighs. Her muffled voice resounded throughout the room. Each lash of the whip drove Jeb deeper into his manic outburst. He wanted to whip her tits and so found a length of chain with a clip, which he placed through the rings in Amy's ankle bracelets and fastened to a ring in the floor. She could not turn now, and guessing his intent, tried to pull her arms down to protect her tender breasts.

Jeb paused a moment, staring at his victim. He looked lustfully on the twin orbs that so invitingly sat ready for the whip. He watched Amy's chest rise and fall as she tried to cope with the pain and humiliation of Jeb's attack. Suddenly, Jeb resumed his assault, striking Amy's breasts blow after blow. Amy screamed in pain behind the cotton sizing of the napkin stuffed so callously in her mouth. Tears streamed down her face as she pulled and yanked at her confinements fruitlessly.

Just as suddenly as he started, Jeb stopped. He was panting from his exertions. He saw the evidence of his rage on Amy's body. He wanted only one thing, now. He wanted to fuck this whore. Loosening the chains on Amy's ankles and wrists, he yelled at her to get to the floor. "On your hands and knees, you slut!" he commanded.

Amy fell to her knees and, leaning over so that her hands touched the floor, arched her back and presented her twin portals to Jeb. "Yes," she thought, "use me, use me!"

Anything to distract Jeb from renewing the painful application of the whip to her body.

Jeb threw the whip to the floor and got down on his knees behind Amy. He pulled his cock from his pants, already steel hard, and pushed it into Amy's anal opening. Amy squealed with pain as her sphincter was stretched and torn. Jeb had fucked her there many times, but always after readying her with his finger, delicately, slowly, widening the entry. As she felt Jeb drive his cock in her to the hilt, she started bucking her ass, hoping to match Jeb's thrusts, to accentuate his pleasure.

"Stay still, you cunt!" Jeb yelled at her. "I'm fucking you!" He slapped his hand down hard on her buttocks, delivering stinging pain to Amy's ass.

As the girl cowered beneath him, Jeb rammed his cock back and forth into her bowels. He drove on relentlessly, slapping his stomach against Amy's rear cheeks. As he started to come, he leaned over Amy's back and grabbed her abused tits. Finding her nipples, he squeezed them hard, causing Amy to moan deeply. As he shot his load into the helpless woman, Jeb felt pulse after pulse of pleasure go through him.

When he was done, Jeb laid across Amy's back, his softening cock still inside her. He had gone through some doorway, entered a forbidden land. He had just beaten a defenseless, frail woman mercilessly because she had talked back to him. He had enjoyed it more than anything he had ever experienced. What had he been missing! As he pushed himself off of the sobbing female, he vowed that this would not be the last time she felt the end of a whip from him.

CHAPTER FIFTEEN

Carmella jumped as she heard the door to the room opening. She heard it close behind her and then slow measured muffled steps across the plush carpet. She could feel the presence of a person behind her. She trembled expectantly. This must be the Prince.

It was the Prince. He was admiring Carmella's delicate, round ass, the gracious curve of her hips, the pale whiteness of her skin. So this was Carmella. He had met her only once, and then she had hidden her charms, or most of them, behind a glittering miniskirt. But now she was here, wearing his mark, standing naked in his rooms.

He circled around her slowly, taking in her delightful body. Her breasts were large, but perfectly proportioned for her frame. Her thighs were well taut and long, her hips wide. Standing in front of her, the Prince gently lifted her breasts, assessing their softness and mass. He flicked his thumbs across the petit, rouged nipples, and watched them stiffen in obedience. Running his hands down her sides, he crouched down so that he could admire the spread of the tattoo that marked her as his property. He bent lower to view the hairless lips of her pussy, the sweet valley between her thighs. Pushing the thighs apart, now kneeling, he licked the length of Carmella's sex, producing a moan from her.

"A luscious whore," he thought, as he delved his tongue past the tender lips and into the moistening gash between them. Carmella sighed, spreading her legs to give her master access to her crevasse. She felt the hot tongue exploring her sheath, the lips pressed against the engorging opening.

The Prince began to suck on the nub of pleasure at the apex of Carmella's sex. It hardened under his oral supplication. Her breath was coming faster, her blood rising. Feeling Carmella's rising desire, the Prince intensified his efforts, lapping at Carmella's clit, driving his tongue deep into her pussy. His hands grabbed her ass and pulled her into his mouth, crushing her pussy against his lips. Pleasure exploded through Carmella's body as her pussy's walls began to throb. She moaned from behind her gag, her knees weakened. She thrust her hips forward, seeking to drive the Prince's expert tongue deeper into her gushing hole.

When he felt Carmella's climax begin to ebb, the Prince rose again to his feet. He wiped his face with a handkerchief, enjoying the erotic scent of Carmella's juices.

Carmella fought half consciously to maintain her feet as the chain pulled her arms up behind her. She steadied herself and regained her footing. It was an unexpected introduction to her erstwhile owner. She fearfully awaited his further pleasure.

"Carmella," the Prince said, "you have a delicious cunt. No wonder so many men are lusting after you."

That voice, where had she heard that voice? She had fucked many men since she had been enslaved, but that voice stood out.

"We have met before, Carmella," the Prince continued, "under different circumstances. I have heard a lot about your talents as a whore and now I know that what I have heard is true. Let me introduce myself, I am Harim Adeem Baroof, but many people call me 'Harry'."

"Harry?" Carmella's mind reeled. Could it be the same man, the man who bought her a drink in the casino so long ago, when she was free, still a real person?

The Prince lifted Carmella's blindfold and looked into her eyes. It was him! "How could this be?" she thought.

"Yes, Carmella, I bought you your last drink as a free woman, many months ago. And just so you know, it was I who alerted the security police that you were fleeing the country. I guessed as much when I saw you leaving after talking to your boyfriend. Jeb was his name, no?"

Carmella's mind reeled as she took this in. He was responsible for her enslavement! He set the police on her! Her eyes widened with hate and fear. This cruel man had taken everything away from her, her dignity, her integrity, her pride. She was a whore because of him. And he had sold her to that monster, Sergi! She tried to fight back the tears, agonized tears that sprung from her memories of that night, her innocence and her betrayal.

"You see, Carmella, I own the casino that your boyfriend robbed," the Prince informed the abject young woman. "You were helping him to escape. But you were worth much more than the money he stole. So I took you instead."

"Jeb, Jeb, Jeb," Carmella thought, "why did you do this to me? How could you have risked me and everything that we had?"

"And it was I who authorized your few days of dalliance at the hotel. The security men telephoned me at once when they had captured you. They told me of your offer to spread your legs for them. It was amusing, an introduction into your new life, as it were. You see, you were a whore even then. You offered up your pussy in exchange for something you wanted. That made you a whore."

Carmella realized that he was right. She had offered her body in exchange for freedom, a quid pro quo. She was a whore. She was always a whore, just waiting for a sufficient price for her cunt.

"You seem to have the ability to bewitch men, Carmella. Aboud was very anxious when he heard you had been sold to Sergi."

Carmella looked up at the Prince in shock.

"Yes, he came here," the Prince continued. "He caused quite a ruckus. He is now sitting in a cell in this very place awaiting my judgment."

"Aboud!" Carmella thought. "He had come to save her! Oh, Aboud, Aboud, I need you!"

The Prince was enjoying his little game. He was stroking her pussy, worrying the little nub of pleasure. In spite of her dismay at the Prince's revelations, Carmella began to grind her hips in reply. "And Sergi has as much as admitted being bewitched. He has offered me a large sum for you. But, tonight you will have the opportunity to bewitch me. Perhaps I will let you stay. Sergi will be disappointed, but no sale is really complete until the goods and money are exchanged."

And Jeb would be there too, the Prince thought to himself. Let him watch as his slut of a fiancé showed her talents. Let's see what stuff he is made of.

"When you are finished your performance tonight, Carmella, you will come to me and suck my cock. Let me feel your talented mouth at work. Convince me that you are a whore worth keeping."

She would convince him. She would use all that she had learned, all of her skills. She looked the Prince in the eyes. "He will want me," she thought.

After the Prince left, Carmella stood confined in the middle of the room for several hours. He had replaced her blindfold and kissed her breasts before leaving. At the end of the third hour, two servants came in and released her. They showed her to the small slaves' bathroom in the Prince's suite where she was able to relieve her bloated bladder. They returned her to her chain, this time locking her hands in front of her and pulling them over her head.

One of the servants carried a latex hood, shiny and black. It fit tightly over Carmella's head and completely blinded her. Her face was covered with the glistening material with holes for her mouth and nose. Carmella felt something pressing against her mouth. It was a circle of rubberized plastic, a ring gag, which popped in and forced her mouth wide open. A long, leather gag was inserted into her oral cavity through the ring and fastened to clips on the mask at either side of her mouth. The gag pressed uncomfortably on the edge of her throat.

The hood went down Carmella's neck almost to her collar. Having her head encased made starker the nakedness of the rest of her body. The blackness of the hood accentuated the paleness of her flesh. The servants left and Carmella again stood alone and in silence.

A short while later, Carmella heard the door to the room open again. She could hear the rattling of bottles and glasses as carts were rolled into the room. After a few moments she could hear the furniture of the room being moved as easy chairs and small tables were arrayed in a semicircle around her.

Carmella heard the familiar swish of chintz skirts as she guessed that pleasure slaves were being led into the room. A rough voice commanded them to kneel by the chairs. She sensed the man step up next to her and then felt a large, muscled hand on her breast. "So this is the entertainment for tonight," the voice said. The voice had the lilt of the English spoken by the Sudanese guards. The hand squeezed Carmella's breast hard, evoking a small moan from her. "I'll be watching you, white cunt. Enjoy yourself."

She heard the man leave and all she could hear was the occasional rustling of skirts and whispers. None of the girl's dared speak loud enough for her to hear. Carmella could smell the women's delicate perfume.

They did not have long to wait until the door opened again and deep Arabic voices were heard. One was the Prince's. There was laughter and banter. Carmella could not tell how many men had entered the room, but she sensed it when several of them stood around her. She could tell that they were admiring her body. She stood tall, with her chest out, her feet turned outwards, her legs spread. This is what she had been taught, what was now bred into her. Her response was automatic.

One of the men bent over and licked Carmella's right breast. Her nipple hardened at the stimulation. A low chuckle was exchanged between the men. The other nipple was licked and it too stiffened obediently.

Jeb had been working at his computer when the Prince called him on the telephone. Amy still lay bound and gagged, as she had for hours after Jeb's savage abuse of her. He had called Rashid and ordered up a cage for her. Later, after it arrived, he would stuff her into it for the night.

The Prince's voice was light and amused. "Paul, I have not seen you for weeks," the Prince said. "I hear that you have been working hard."

"Yes, Prince, I have some good numbers to show you. I…."

"I am sure that you do, Paul, but I didn't call for that. I am having an entertainment in my suite at about 8:30. Please come, you will enjoy it immensely."

A request from the Prince was a command.

"Certainly, my Prince," Jeb responded, "I'll be there."

There was no doubt in Jeb's mind that this entertainment involved the torture and abuse of a luckless slave. He was in the mood for that. And when he came back, he thought, he would whip Amy again.

Jeb was surprised to see the Prince's suite filled with seven or eight swarthy Arabs. They were dressed like the Prince normally did, late collegiate. A girl was in the middle of the room, her hands extended into the air, a latex hood over her head. The entertainment, he thought. He walked up to her, admiring her graceful form and sweet tits. The mark of Adeem was across her stomach, classifying her as a pleasure slave. Jeb saw the golden disc at her loins. Her name would be on it. But what difference did her name make? She was a whore and a cunt like all the rest.

The Prince saw Jeb admiring Carmella's body. It was thinner than when she was captured and the way she had been trained to present her body was certainly something she had not practiced when she and Jeb had been together. Only if he examined her tag would a suspicion creep into Jeb's mind. But, as he had anticipated, Jeb was too inured to the life of a slave master to care about her name.

The men were all enjoying their drinks and conversation. Carmella could hear an occasional voice in English, but the subtle din of the room obscured most of the words. She was nervous. She knew from the trouble that the Prince had gone to that her 'entertainment' of these men would involve some special torment for her. She was sweating inside the tight hood. Her arms ached from their extreme extension, her legs were cramping. As the time went on, the cold pit in Carmella's stomach grew deeper and deeper.

The Prince called out in Arabic to the men. Jeb had been talking to one of them, a young, dark man, small, but well built. His hair was black and he wore Gucci loafers and a pink Izod shirt. He identified himself as the owner of a small "house" nearby the House of Adeem. He greatly admired the Prince and what he had done for the slave trade in Calipha. They were all getting rich off of the bodies of these white sluts.

The man asked Jeb what he did for the Prince. Jeb was uncertain what he was permitted to reveal and so he gave a generalized answer, something about financial advice.

"You must advise me!" the man exclaimed. "Oh, I will talk to the Prince. My whores are not the class of his, of course, but they are obedient and willing. Come and be my guest. You will think you are in heaven. And then we can talk about financial matters. Not too much though!" He smiled conspiratorially.

"Come now, Paul, the entertainment is about to begin. Take a seat near me," the Prince called out to Jeb invitingly.

Jeb knew that the Prince's chair would be nearest to where the action was and so he readily agreed.

As he sat down, the lights in the room dimmed. He felt the presence of a pleasure slave at his knees. If this turned out the way he believed it would, he would have need of her services shortly.

The room quieted as a broad beamed spotlight shown down upon Carmella. She did not notice it, but she did notice the room quieting. Whatever was going to happen to her was going to happen now.

Jeb saw a slight, Asian man step into the spotlight. He was naked except for a small loincloth. He was at least 30, maybe 35. His black hair was cut short. He bowed to the audience. The Prince stood up an introduced him.

"Please, my guests, I would like to introduce for you Mr. Chu Ling," the Prince announced. A smattering of applause rose from the audience. "He is the master of the needle as an instrument of pain and he has come to Calipha to purchase some new subjects for his show in Bangkok."

Carmella could hear every word that the Prince was saying. She realized that she was about to be subjected to a new form of excruciating pain. Nervously, she began to tug at her chains. She had wanted to remain stoic through as much of the abuse that she anticipated as possible. But this use of needles portended a level of pain that she was wholly unprepared for. Despite herself, she began to emit a small whine.

The Prince continued his introduction of Mr. Ling, taking no notice of Carmella's discomfort.

"He has graciously agreed to give us a little demonstration of his art. I promise that you will enjoy it."

Jeb glowed with anticipation. He had noted, with some amusement, the discomfiture of the strung up slave who was to be the subject of Mr. Ling's attentions. He wondered if he would get to fuck her later.

Mr. Ling bowed and expressed his thanks to the Prince. As the Prince resumed his seat, a servant brought a small table over to Mr. Ling. On the table was a long, thin, black leather case. Lowly amplified Eastern style music began to play in the room. "This exercise is called the Dance of the Seven Needles," Mr. Ling announced to the crowd. He bowed again and turned to face Carmella.

There was a hushed silence as Mr. Ling advanced towards Carmella and pressed his body up against hers. Carmella was shaking with fear and she vainly tried to pull her body away from him. She could feel the hardness of his cock as it pressed against her stomach. He ran his hands down her back and over her rear. His mouth was next to her ear and Carmella could hear him chanting in a low, sonorous voice. The words were Chinese, an apparent necessary part of the ritual. Despite her panicked state, Carmella began to be mesmerized by the indecipherable words.

Mr. Ling moved to the rear of Carmella. Now his caresses could be seen by the audience. They watched his hands circle Carmella's tits and gently squeeze them. As he held her, he began a swaying motion with his body, taking Carmella with him. Carmella could feel the warmth of the man's body as it pressed against her. That, and the experience of having her breasts stroked and caressed before this appreciative crowd, stoked her passion. She fell deeper into a trance-like state as the man's hands left her breasts and ran down her stomach to her sex below.

Rubbing his hands along the inside of Carmella's pale, tender thighs, Mr. Ling resumed his incantations. All eyes were on the rocking, swaying couple. Ling started to caress Carmella's pussy, pulling the excited lips apart and plunging his fingers inside. Sensing Carmella's rising lust, he raised his hands and loosened the clasps that held the long, hard, gag in Carmella's mouth, removing it but leaving the mouth-spreading ring in place. The low, deep-pitched moans that had been emerging from Carmella's throat became louder, almost amplified.

Ling stepped away to the table, opened the small, rectangular case that lay there and produced a three-inch long, steel needle embedded in a small, round disc, about an inch and a half in thickness.

Ling walked across the front of the circle of light surrounding Carmella holding the torture device up so that the audience could see it. Blinded by the hood, all Carmella knew was that his caresses had stopped. Her pussy was burning with desire. She could feel it, open and wet with her fluids.

Jeb focused intently on the dripping slit. Hairless and smooth, it captivated him. His cock was already rock hard and the show had barely begun. His gaze left the unfortunate woman's crotch as he noticed the shiny device in Mr. Ling's hand. He wondered where it would go.

"The first needle!" Mr. Ling exclaimed. He circled behind Carmella and, placing his back against hers, lifted one of her feet. Carmella was jolted out of her induced state of semi-consciousness. Something was about to happen.

Ling trapped Carmella's leg between his own. Fruitlessly, she tried to pull it away, aware that some painful thing was about to be done to her foot. The bottom of her foot was exposed to Ling's darks design. He felt along it one with one hand as he held the embedded needle in his other. When he was satisfied that he had found the precise location of his search, a spot just at the end of the heel and the beginning of the sole, Ling pressed the sharp point of the needle into Carmella's foot.

The ring gag prevented the formation of any words from Carmella, but it did not suppress sounds. Carmella screamed out in pain as the needle found the nerve Ling was seeking. Ling waited for Carmella's cry of pain to subside, and then he twisted the needle in her foot, drawing renewed howls of pain from Carmella. Three times he let her voice rise and fall. Satisfied, he gently let her foot down to the floor.

The needle was not in all the way. There was enough left outside Carmella's foot that any pressure on the pin drove it deeper, exacerbating the sharp pain. When Carmella put down her foot, she was forced to her toes as the slightest downward pressure of her heel produced exquisite pain.

Ling produced a similarly configured needle from the black case on the table and showed it to the audience.

"Needle two," he called.

Carmella, and everyone else, knew precisely where the next needle would go. Ling captured Carmella's left foot and repeated the exercise he had performed on the right. It produced the same agonized cry from Carmella. When he let the foot down, after causing repeated moaning outbursts from the helpless female by manipulating the needle, Carmella was forced to her toes on both feet.

Another needle was produced, this one without a base, but clubbed at one end. It was about seven inches long. Ling stepped in front of Carmella and began to lick and suck at her right tit. She, of course, had not seen the ominous looking needle, but knew that her breasts were the targets of the cruel Asian's next assault.

Strangely, the pain in Carmella's feet, together with her apprehension about the next insertion, caused Carmella's feet begin to step up and down. The increments were small, her feet lifting no more than a few millimeters off of the floor. But it did seem that she was doing a dance.

The next needle pressed home directly through the tip of Carmella's right nipple. Carmella felt the piercing pain as her breast was violated by the long steel weapon. Expertly, Ling pressed it in until the needle met the wall of Carmella's chest. Carmella was now mindless, conscious only of pain. Her howls were loud and long. When the left one went in, after a ceremonious announcement of "needle four!" by Ling, she literally gurgled with agony. The hopping of her feet intensified. When Ling stepped back from her body, someone shouted out, "Look, she's dancing!" A round of applause circled the room.

And so she was. The pain was so excruciating that it was causing spasms in Carmella's thighs. Her body wanted rest, to place her feet on the ground, but each time her heel fell, a jolt of pain shot up her leg causing the other foot to rise as she tried to regain her toes.

Needles five and six were for Carmella's pussy. Ling knelt between Carmella's thighs and gently spread them. She was able to keep off her heels only by cooperating by widening her legs. Ling, before inserting the needles, took some time to lick and suck at the gaping hole. Carmella could no more ignore the pleasure from his mouth than she could ignore the pain from the needles. She let out a deep, soulful moan of frustration and pain. When Ling was satisfied that the tunnel of her sex was sufficiently lubricated and distended, he showed the needle to the crowd and announced, "Needle five!"

The needle was about eight inches long. It reached far into Carmella's canal, pressing against a nerve deep inside her womb. The other needle proceeded soon after the first. Carmella's body was in a frenzy. Her involuntary dancing became more intense, her howls of pain, continuous.

Jeb was, as were all the men, virtually entranced by Carmella's suffering. He grabbed the head of the slave kneeling next to him and pulled her to his loins. Terrified by Carmella's brutal torture, the girl quickly opened his fly and drew out his rock hard tool. She engulfed it with her mouth, only too glad that she no longer had to watch the terrible spectacle of Carmella's debasement.

Ling circled the light once again and held out a needle about three inches long. He smiled as he did so, knowing full well the rapture of his audience. "Needle seven," he exclaimed.

The man knelt at Carmella's feet and squeezed the fulcrum of her sex. When the little bud had grown stiff, he plunged the needle in just below it, piercing the nerve that lay at its base. He stepped away, letting the audience appreciate the product of his art. Carmella's whole body trembled, her voice reduced to a steady, piteous whine. Her feet danced as her body sought to process seven points of excruciating pain.

Ling now drew off his loincloth. His cock was rampant as was every cock in the room. He paused for a few moments, allowing the audience to take in the physical evidence of Carmella's torment. She jerked and spasmed in a cruel parody of a dance. Her sensory system was overloaded. The pain was like a river flowing through her. In a voice understandable by no one, she begged and pleaded for mercy.

Ling circled again behind Carmella and spread the cheeks of her ass. Slowly he eased his prick into her bowels. Carmella's voice modulated at this new sensation. Something inside her told her that this was the beginning of the end. Frantically, she began to throw her ass back at her tormentor. She squeezed the cock as hard as she could with her sphincter muscles.

Jeb could see Ling's appreciative face over Carmella's shoulder. Her screams of pain and her tortured dance spurred his lust. The expert mouth surrounding his cock slowly and patiently manipulated him. He could hear the sounds of men's gasps of pleasure throughout the room. He grabbed the head of the slave who tantalized his cock. He wanted to come when Ling did. He moved the head of the slave in time with Ling's thrusts.

As he slowly pistoned in and out of Carmella's ass, Ling aggravated the needles that pierced Carmella's flesh. He measured his thrusts against her outpouring of pain. When he felt that she had reached the apex of her tolerance, he pushed hard inside her bowels and came.

Her heart leapt with glee as Carmella felt the cock throbbing in her ass. It would soon be over! Unconsciously, she continued to howl and scream with pain to the immeasurable delight of the callous men in the room. But her mind felt the diminishing pulses of the cock that pierced her and she rejoiced.

Jeb had timed his climax perfectly. He could see the Asian man's face contract as he shot his sperm deep into the slave girl. At the same time, Jeb's cock spurted his load into the mouth of the nameless slave between his thighs.

Ling withdrew from Carmella's ass and ceased his manipulation of the seven piercings of Carmella's body. All around the room was the sound of male orgasms, as they were brought off by the mouths of fearful, trembling slaves. He waited for the sounds to subside. Carmella was still twitching and moaning, her feet nervously tapping the floor. When he knew he again had the attention of the audience, Ling quickly withdrew the seven tortuous needles from Carmella's body. He did them in reverse order and, after he pulled the last needle from Carmella's right foot, he advanced to the audience and bowed.

The room resounded with the applause and cheers of the now well-satisfied men. Ling bowed twice to the audience and, in a moment that the Prince had been waiting for, reached back and removed Carmella's mask.

A second round of applause sounded throughout the room. Carmella, through her lingering pain, felt that this round of applause was for her, recognition of her 'delightful' suffering. Straining, she raised her head, peering out to the audience. The spotlight was blinding, but she sensed the wildness of the men. She had performed for the Prince. His guests were well pleasured. Inwardly, she smiled.

Jeb, however, had a totally different response to the termination of the show. He looked intently at the limply hanging girl. It couldn't be! His mind was playing tricks on him! It looked like... it had to be... Carmella! Jeb's body became stone cold. At all once, it dawned on him that he had applauded and cheered for the most excruciating torture he had ever witnessed, and the victim of the torture was his lost lover, Carmella.

At that moment, a stone formed in his heart. What had he become? He was too stunned to move, too stunned to react. "Carmella, Carmella, Carmella," he thought, "what have I done to you?"

Meanwhile Carmella was recovering her senses. Her moans were now reduced to tears, her shaking subsided. She felt her hands released from the chain above her head and she fell to the floor. Her muscles were like rubber. But it was over! She had survived once again! Then she remembered that she had one more job to do.

Carmella crawled forwards. She knew that the Prince would be at the center of the crowd, that he would be waiting for her. Hands fastened her wrists behind her back, but still she squirmed forwards, seeking her master. As she passed from the circle of light, she saw him sitting, his legs spread wide, his cock rampant and protruding, awaiting her lips.

Slowly, Carmella traversed the distance between the arc of light and the Prince. When she reached him, she fought herself to her knees and edged herself forward between his thighs. She found his cock with her mouth and pressed it deep within, to the edge of her throat.

A crowd had gathered around them now, as they pressed in to watch the culmination of the night's entertainment. They began to clap rhythmically and sing in Arabic as they urged Carmella on.

Her mouth was still distended by the ring gag, but her tongue and her throat were enough to drive the passion of the Prince. He was as affected as any man in the room, and his cock was primed to explode. The pressure of Carmella's throat on the head of his thick, steel hard prick was enough to spark his orgasm. He held her head tightly to his loins and groaned.

The other men in the room, all except Jeb, yelled and cheered as they witnessed the Prince's climax.

CHAPTER SIXTEEN

That evening and for the next two days, Carmella was allowed to sleep. She was exhausted from her ordeal and was kept in the infirmary so that her wounds could heal. Ling came to see her and thank her for her performance. When she saw him, she shuddered and had no reply since she was kept gagged while she recuperated.

Mr. Ling was an expert at his devilish art and the punctures inside her womb were actually quite minute, the needles having been inserted just deep enough to press on the nerve endings that the cruel man sought. The wounds in her breasts were very deep, but again, being the master of his craft, Ling had made the needles operating room clean before their use. He had worn barely perceptible, translucent latex gloves during the procedure.

And so on the third day after her ordeal, Carmella was declared by the Mansion's physician in residence as being available for use.

After being released from the infirmary, Carmella was taken, bound, gagged and hooded back to the Prince's suite. She was led into the bedroom, a sumptuous room with fine golden draperies, a thick Persian rug and heavy, deep maroon, mahogany furniture. She was able to take in the fine appointments of the room when her hood was removed. She was to become minutely familiar with its details over the next two weeks.

The servant who had led her to the Prince's bedroom, after removing her hood, walked her over to a small bathroom, obviously designed for use by the Prince's female servants. There was a bidet and a toilet and a small sink and shower. Carmella was ordered to bathe herself and to use the facilities. She was surprised when the servant unlocked her leather bracelets and collar and removed them from the room.

Luxuriating in the warmth of the shower and the freedom of her body, Carmella lingered under the streams of hot water. How different from the showers in the dungeons of the House of Adeem. When she emerged from the shower she dried herself off with a plush cotton towel. Her hair was still short and so needed only a brief scruffing with the towel to absorb the wetness and a few pulls of the brush that was provided to straighten it. She perfumed herself lightly from the atomizer on the counter and then knocked on the bathroom door to signal that she was done.

When she emerged, a servant was standing next to the Prince's bed waiting for her. Carmella looked with dismay at what could only be intended as the new accouterments for her body. A shiny, heavy steel collar lay on the bed together with four similar bracelets. A thick, black leather gag sat next to them. The servant who stood there was not the same one who had led her in and Carmella assumed that this was the Prince's personal batman, commander of the Prince's rooms when he was not present. He was holding a rattan cane in his hand.

Carmella was about to speak when the cane came swinging towards her, striking her on the thigh, drawing a moan of pain from her. "No talking!" the servant commanded. He was wearing the same unformed white coat worn by the other servants, but his was decorated with gold piping along the collar and a gold and black woven insignia over the right breast, the Prince's coat of arms.

The slender, short, brown skinned man ordered Carmella to present her wrists to him. He locked a steel bracelet on each wrist. Carmella could feel the weight of the confinements immediately. When her ankles had been secured, the man had Carmella kneel and applied her collar. It weighed heavily on her neck. While she had often been able to forget that she had constantly been attired in bindings designed to ease her confinement and control, these would not easily be ignored. The servant bound Carmella's hands behind her back.

Next came the gag. It consisted of a large leather wedge, designed to spread the jaws, covered by a thin sheath of shiny black leather. It was embossed on the front with the Prince's crest. Its tapered end was long enough to reach to the back of the mouth. It was obviously designed to produce both discomfort and silence. Carmella desperately wanted to refuse the gag, but she knew better. It would be forced in one way or another and the least struggle on her part would certainly result in a beating. She obediently opened her mouth and the thick leather was forced in.

The gag pressed down on her tongue and forced her to spread her lips wide. The leather sheath covered the bottom portion of her face and was supple enough to fall flat against her cheeks when the straps were fastened behind her head. She would be virtually unrecognizable while wearing the gag. It was clearly designed to depersonalize the wearer. Carmella had been at peace over the last couple of days, although she was still panicked at the thought that she might be soon shipped off to the clutches of Sergi. The application of these dramatic new bindings and confinements on her shattered that peace.

Standing there obediently, Carmella awaited the next development. She expected to be bound to the foot of the Prince's bed, as she had been bound to many beds many times before while awaiting her use. She learned that her assumption was wrong when she saw a rectangular Plexiglas box being wheeled into the room. It had large holes in it on the sides, near the bottom. It was just large enough for a woman to kneel in with her back bent over, crushing her breasts against her knees.

The small, silent man pulled the box over to where Carmella stood and, unfastening clips along the bottom, pulled the Plexiglas cover free. He commanded her to kneel on the platform. It was covered with a felt lining over a thick pad and was soft on her knees as Carmella tearfully let herself down onto it. Her ankles bracelets were clipped to small rings on either side of the base, spreading her legs about the width of her body.

The servant came around to the front and attached a short, light chain to the front of her collar and pulled her head down towards the base. He clipped it to a strategically placed ring. Carmella was now held tightly in place. She heard the Plexiglas cover being lifted and felt it around her sides as the servant maneuvered it in place. Before lowering it, he clipped another small chain to the back of the gag. He threaded it through the top and as the Plexiglas was lowered, Carmella's head was pulled up straight. She could move her head up or down only a few inches and just a little bit more side to side. She was pinioned so that she was forced to look forwards, a perfect presentation position.

The servant was not finished. He wheeled the box over to the wall opposite the foot of the bed. He backed it up about three feet from the wall so that Carmella had a clear view of the massive footboard. He stood next to the box and Carmella could feel him pumping at something beneath her. The box started to rise on its frame. It swayed slightly as it was ratcheted upwards in small jerks. When the bottom of the box had reached the level of the mattress, the servant ceased pumping and locked the frame in place.

There was an opening in the rear of the box large enough for a man to insert a hand. The servant stepped to the opening and reached in. The manner in which Carmella was mounted, her legs spread apart about a foot and a half, left her sex readily accessible. She felt the servant's hand begin to stroke her pussy. He was evidently skilled as he soon had Carmella's cunt glistening with moisture. He took his time, gently stroking the naked lips, fingering the clit. Carmella's view was of her master's bed. On the wall above the headboard was a carved rendition of his crest, a black falcon, wings extended, set over a pair of crossed scimitars. The hilts of the swords were red, the blades silver. Broad gold and green pennants swept below and above. Black Arabic writing formed a semicircle underneath.

This was Carmella's enforced view as the servant's hand enflamed her passion. Carmella did not want to respond. She hated herself for it. But she had been trained well and it took little more than a touch to lubricate her and to ultimately bring her to orgasm.

Carmella could hear the echo of her strained breathing inside the clear glass container as she gave in to the relentless hand between her thighs. Her confined thighs began to jerk and she tried to press her turgid loins down upon the hand. Her pussy began to throb and she came hard, moaning and straining at her bonds.

As she recovered from her orgasm. Carmella hardly noticed as the man brought a gold cotton cloth and draped it around the top of the frame, covering its metal parts all the way to the floor. The box was then pushed back against the wall. He had one last thing to do. He stepped away and returned with a four inch high and 2 foot long plaque. He showed it to the helpless woman. It was black and had her name written across it in large golden scriptive letters, "CARMELLA". The servant smiled at her as he slid it into two grooves at the front base of the Plexiglas box.

For the next two weeks this was to be Carmella's home. She was released twice during the course of each day, and at least once during the evening. Each time she was massaged, showered, allowed to eat, empty her bowels and then returned to the presentation case. Each time that the room was entered, for cleaning, for the drawing of the curtains and the lighting of the dim lamps embedded in sconces along the walls in the evening, for any purpose whatsoever, Carmella's stand would be wheeled away from the wall and she would be stroked and caressed until she came. After the third or fourth time, her pussy began to moisten as soon as she heard the door opening. She would watch intently as the servants or serving slaves moved about the room knowing that soon a hand would reach in behind her and bring her to pleasure. Often, if more than one servant had come into the room, or if the servant had ordered a slave to caress her, she would be watched lustfully as her body was driven relentlessly to sexual climax.

The rest of the time, Carmella knelt unhappily waiting for time to go by. Her vision was limited to that which was right before her and the crest of the Prince was always within her gaze. She became intricately familiar with its every detail.

The Prince had, grudgingly, determined that a deal was a deal and that he would have to give her over to Sergi when he returned to Calipha at the end of the two weeks. But he had decided to enjoy her as much as he could for as long as he could in the meantime. Carmella still hoped against hope that he would not sell her. The Prince purposely kept her in ignorance for he knew that when he used her she would be at the peak of her exertions to prove her worth.

In the meantime, he enjoyed seeing her piteous, frantic eyes whenever he came into the room. She would follow his every movement as he went about. His revenge was complete. Jeb had confessed tearfully the day after Carmella was tortured before his very eyes. He begged and pleaded for her release. When the Prince refused, he begged to see her just once. The Prince said no. The man was a wreck, and since he would be of no use to anyone until he recovered, the Prince had him cast into a cell in the vast basement of the mansion, ironically, right next to Aboud. Perhaps they would compare notes on Carmella. This amused the Prince. The two men would hate each other, one for the other's abandonment of Carmella, the other for what he had made her become. And Carmella was headed for what was, in very real terms, a fate worse than death.

On the evening of the first day that Carmella had been trapped in her prison of glass, he came in just after dusk to admire what was still, technically, his property. The glass was sparkling clean and Carmella's form was brightly lit by a small overhead lamp. He stood in front of her admiring her graceful curves and appreciating her distressed look. She had not spoken an intelligible word to anyone since she had left the House of Adeem. The Prince was determined that she would remain speechless until she was shipped off to her new owner. Thus, she would not be even given the opportunity to beg for deliverance from her cruel fate.

On that first night, he had ordered her removed from the box. He had stripped naked and awaited her on his bed as the frame was lowered by his manservant and she was brought to him. Her hands remained bound behind her as she crawled onto the bed. The Prince had ordered that no one was to talk to her other than to issue curt commands when the need be. He maintained his own silence except to tell her how to arrange her body or when to get off of the bed.

He was laying on his back, his cock already hard when she approached him on her knees. He ordered her to straddle him and to impale herself on his manhood. She was already wet and had little difficulty in pushing the hot cock up inside her. She needed no instruction to begin arching her hips, pushing herself up and down with her knees to provide friction for her master's tool. She gazed at him imploringly as she rode his prick, knowing full well that it was he who had ordered her cruel confinement.

The Prince enjoyed seeing his mark on her belly, his crest on the outer covering of the gag that she wore. He reached out and caressed the breasts that he owned. Few men are as fortunate as I, he thought. Carmella was a well trained whore and she squeezed his cock with the muscles of her quim as she caressed him with the length of her sheath. She could sense his impending climax and rode him harder, bringing her own lust to a boil. When she felt his hot sperm shoot deep inside her, she came, moaning and crying from behind her gag.

Many nights the Prince used her. Except when she was ordered to suck his cock she was always gagged. And the use of her arms and hands was always denied her. He had ordered that, even when being bathed, her arms should remain locked behind. She never spent the night in his bed. Each time, when he was finished with her, he would order the ever present servant to return her to her presentation case. The light over her was kept on during the night so that, if he awakened before the morning, he could see her kneeling naked and helpless before him.

On some nights he did not use her. After all, he had hundreds of slaves to choose from. He let her watch as he plowed this cunt or that. He had grown fond of Mrs. Paralova and several nights during this period he had enjoyed her enthusiastic fucking. When he had another slave, or slaves, in his bed, a servant would stand behind Carmella and stroke her pussy. She would come repeatedly as she watched her master lustfully enjoy his other property.

Carmella had been a big hit the night of her entertainment. The Prince acquiesced in the demands of his friends and colleagues to fuck her. So on a number of occasions, Carmella would be wheeled through the hallways of the mansion to the bedroom of a guest. The case would be covered with a cloth during her transport and the Prince had ordered that her gag should not be removed by anyone. He reserved the use of her mouth to himself.

Carmella was not whipped once during this period. She was grateful enough for that. Her time was divided between periods of almost insufferable boredom and exquisite pleasure. She began to yearn for the door to open to be allowed to feel pleasure. Her period of freedom from her box was so limited that she rejoiced any time that she was used or during her thrice daily washings and feedings. She was fed water through a tube that could be inserted in a small hole in the gag. She was not even removed from the box to urinate. A servant would simply place a bowl between her knees and order her to piss. She would obey or spend time later, in agony, as her bladder, cramped by the pressure of her stomach, filled to near bursting.

Only once did she refuse to obey the command to return to her tiny prison. She had been showered and fed, the servant spooning a nutritious mush to her. She often cried during the day and she had been crying that morning. When the servant urged her towards her hateful confinement she had pulled against the chain, struggling to avoid her encapsulation. The servant calmly took hold of her nose and cut off her supply of air. As Carmella began to suffocate, she whined and cried to induce the servant to let go. He waited until her eyes began to flutter to release her nose and permit her to take a breath. Afterwards, she meekly permitted herself to be returned to her Plexiglas prison.

Carmella had plenty of time to think. Her thoughts concentrated on two main themes. She cursed her fate and what she had become. Jennine was right. She was nothing more than a pet. Her current torment was indisputable proof of that. She was not just denied speech, she was denied the ability to speak. She was petted and cared for and used at the discretion of her owner and master. She was a human animal who could perform pleasurable tricks.

The other principle thought in her mind was fear for the future. Somehow, the fact that the Prince had taken so much trouble to display and mount her in his room gave her encouragement. She had performed well for him on the night of her torture and had done so since. The Prince had virtually not said a word to her since that night, but couldn't that mean that he had decided to keep her? Or did it mean the opposite, that he was dehumanizing her so that he could easily ship her off when the time came?

It was midmorning that they came for her. She had been wheeled from the Prince's room, as she had on other occasions. She was rolled onto the elevator as she had been before when she was taken upstairs to the guest's rooms. But this time the elevator went, not up, but down.

Carmella knew that down was bad. She had remained on the upper floors since she had been brought here. She remembered being dragged though the basement when she arrived. She knew that she was leaving.

As soon as she felt the elevator begin to descend, Carmella felt as if an icy knife had been driven into her stomach. She began to shake and moan in her box in a frantic protest against her fate. When the box was taken off of the elevator and wheeled a short distance, the cloth covering was removed and Carmella saw two of the menacing black guards standing next to her. The Plexiglas cover was lifted and she felt the cool, damp air of the cellar. Her ankles and neck were released and she was gruffly pulled to her feet. Futilely, she cried and struggled. She tried to kick the hands away that were connecting her ankles together. The gag that had silenced her for a fortnight was removed and Carmella cried out forlornly, "Please, no, don't take me away! Please don't do this, please!" Those were the only words that she had the opportunity to say as the traveling hood was pulled over her head and its wedge of leather stuffed into her mouth.

Carmella was dragged, still struggling, from the basement and outside to a waiting van. She was quickly subdued inside, her ankles locked to her wrists. The van sped away. As it rolled along the desert highway, Carmella continued to rail against her fate. She knew that Sergi, unrestricted by the even very liberal rules at the House of Adeem would inflict woeful tortures on her. What had happened to those who loved her? Aboud had tried to save her, where was he now? And Jeb, had he done anything to free her? Was she worthless except as a creature to be debased, used as a receptacle for lust?

When the van finally slowed and pulled to a halt, Carmella had resigned herself to her fate. What else did life have in store for her anyway? Let it happen. She knew she would not last long for she had no will to live. Let him kill her. He would be doing her a favor.

Carmella felt herself dragged from the van. Despite her resignation, she was limp with fear with the thought that within minutes, seconds, she would be under Sergi's power. She was taken down a small set of stairs, through a doorway and down a long corridor. She heard a heavy door opening and she was pulled inside and thrown to her knees. A hand held her head up while another worked at loosening the hood. First her mouth was freed and then her eyes. She looked up fearfully. Aboud!

EPILOGUE

The Prince sat in a wooden lawn chair located in the shade of a tall palm tree. He was watching the exercise of his thoroughbreds. Horse racing was his second passion. He had several new, promising acquisitions. He was determined to win the annual Caliphate Cup this spring. Although he was the Prince and could do almost literally anything that he wanted, including fixing horse races, he was a man of honor and a gentleman, and such things simply were not done.

He chuckled to himself bemusedly as he contemplated the ironies of fate. Two days before Carmella was destined to be sent to her terrible fate, Rashid had come into his office at the mansion. He was dragging along the little slave that had been acquired as a potential assistant to Jeb. She had a chain connecting her ankles, restricting her movement and she had to scurry to keep up with him.

Rashid had enjoyed himself with this slut and had magnified and multiplied her piercings. Large brass rings now descended from her nose and her breasts. She wore a chain of little bells between her legs, fastened to a heavy ring through her clit. Her ears had been ringed repeatedly and each ring had dangling from it another little bell. The bells were of varying sizes and weights and so a melodious cacophony followed her wherever she went. A heavy weight hung from her pierced tongue, forcing it to dangle outside of her mouth. At the end of it was another bell.

Rashid was laughing as he entered the room. Rashid seldom laughed and the Prince wondered what had caused this unusual event.

"Oh, Great One, I bring you terrible news," he said when he could catch his breath.

"Don't give me that 'Oh, Great One" routine," the Prince replied, annoyed. "Do you always laugh at terrible news?"

"No, your Highness, no. But it seems that fate has taken a hand. Sergi Krasjnavic has been shot." He started laughing again.

"Sergi, my partner, has been shot and you laugh!" the Prince exclaimed.

"Oh, don't worry, your Highness, his lieutenant, a Mr. Jakov, has assumed the responsibilities under Mr. Sergi's contracts and all will be as before. He has graciously relieved you of any obligation you had to Mr. Krasjnavic and is sending another boatload of beauties as a gesture of his good will. General Blasic has given Mr. Jakov his blessing, and money and slaves will flow as anticipated."

The Prince hesitated and then, perceiving the irony of the situation also began to laugh. The two grown men, slavers and cruel tormentors of women, laughed uncontrollably for almost ten minutes.

Finally, the Prince tried to bring himself under control. "That means, ha, ha, that Carmella, ha, ha, ha, ha, ha, ha, ha!" He broke out again in a belly laugh. Tears were coming to his eyes.

When the men finally calmed down they began to discuss the implications of this incredible news.

"Who shot him?" the Prince asked, suppressing his humor.

"Why, Mr. Jakov, of course," Rashid replied. "He discovered that Mr. Krasjnavic had diverted some valuable assets to you for his own benefit. I believe the reference is to Mrs. Paralova and her lovely daughters. And that certain credits due to him and his confederates had been converted by Mr. Krasjnavic to use as consideration for his application to 'retire' here."

"Well, he got his wish," the Prince wryly remarked. "He is certainly retired."

The men laughed again.

Rashid left, still chuckling to himself.

So now the Prince had a dilemma. What was he to do with Carmella? He had found himself falling under her bewitching spell. If he could, he would keep her mounted in his bedroom indefinitely. But eventually the effect of being so confined would tell on her. She was a beautiful, skilled whore, and deserved a better fate than that.

And then there was the problem of Aboud. He was an experienced and dedicated master trainer of slaves. They were not that easily found. After giving it much thought, the Prince decided to allow Aboud to have Carmella as his body slave. Call it a gesture to love. Undoubtedly, Aboud would eventually tire of her and she would return to her status as a mere whore. In the meantime, he would make it absolutely clear that she remained his property, to do with as he would. And, she must serve, in one way or another.

As it turned out, Aboud began to use Carmella as an assistant in his training regimen. She helped him feed and water the new girls and even beat them from time to time. At least once a week she served above ground, usually as a gift to a special guest. He could not send her to the second floor, where Jennine awaited her, angered that her taunts of Carmella had come to naught. In fact, she made quite a scene. Perhaps it was time for a change in management. That Mexican drug lord, Manuel Perez, had more than once made quite generous offers for Jennine. The Prince was sure he could find an excuse to file a criminal charge against her. She too would then be "stung on the hand". He might let Aboud and Carmella train her. The Prince enjoyed ironies.

And Jeb. What to do with Jeb? The man was a financial wizard. The two million dollars he had given Jeb to 'play with' had grown, within a few months, to three. And the financial reforms he had urged on the Prince had turned out very well, adding significantly to the Prince's coffers.

About a week after he had sent Carmella to Aboud, the Prince had Jeb brought up and had a long talk with him. The Prince was a master of seduction and it did not take long to convince Jeb that he was better off without that slut, Carmella. He proffered Jeb his old position back and the restoration of his slave privileges, including the whore Amy. Within a week, Jeb was his old self and back to making money for the Prince.

The Prince sipped his iced tea as one of his new animals dashed by, urged on by a talented jockey. He missed the opportunity to fuck and torment Carmella, but he was enjoying more and more the use of the former Mrs. Kristina Paralova. He had held on to the three sisters and they were still virgins, at least technically. He had used their other orifices well. Perhaps he would marry them. He needed an heir and they would produce beauteous offspring. Between the three of them they should produce at least one son. And the mother would be there to care for the children. He would have to make sure that their vocal cords were cut. There was nothing worse than the prospect of a nagging wife, not to mention three of them.

Yes, it was good to be the Prince.

* * * * * *

Sixty miles across the desert, as the falcon flies, a slim, dark haired girl was twisting and turning at the end of a chain, trying to assuage the impact of the blows of a short rattan cane. The cane was in the hand of Carmella and they, along with her master, Aboud, were in his private suite beneath the whorehouse known as the House of Adeem. Carmella had waited long for this moment, as this was the girl who was responsible for a beating she had received, many months ago. Carmella stood, naked and sweating, having finally been satisfied that the girl had been repaid. Aboud was sitting on his bed, looking on approvingly. Seeing that Carmella was done, he called out to her, "Whore, come here and suck my prick."

She smiled at him and came onto his bed.

The End